Elision.

<u>**OTHER KOKOPELLIMA PRESS BOOKS BY ANGEL BRYNNER**</u>

Eutaxis   Ecclesia   Exodus

Erebus   Exist   Esthesis   Epicharis

Elision   Elysum   Empyrean

<u>**AOLAB active art decks & books BY ANGEL BRYNNER**</u>

ZION   HALCYON   DELUGE   BLOOD OF MY BLOOD

FLESH OF MY FLESH   BONE OF MY BONE

BLACKWATER   OVERFLOW   EDEN   ZENITH

<u>**AOLAB Travelogues BY ANGEL BRYNNER**</u>

BOTTOM OF THE NINTH WARD BULLETINS

BLACKWATER RISING

<u>**Anthologies BY ANGEL BRYNNER**</u>

FIRESTARTER   FIREWALKER

Elision.

/grievechronic\

Angel Brynner

KOKOPELLIMA PRESS

Library of Congress
Cataloging-in-Publication Data
Brynner, Angel
Elision, grievechronic/ Angel Brynner
Library of Congress control number:2019956842
ISBN: 978-1-950077-06-9
EBOOK ISBN 978-1-950077-07-6

Cover artwork and book design by AOLAB
Additional artwork designed by toppng
Website : http://www.GRIEVECHRONIC.com

KokoPelliMa Press

**...For Love. Period.
In the fire, and finally in the rain.**

...And for the will to fight back.

**Sometimes the things done in death
become the closest to "living out loud"
that we get tricked into settling for.**

"But if the light of the eye is darkness…"

Elision

chapter one

Thyaz was hovering over Artyo when she came to.

She turned her head and began to cough out bloody bullets as he pushed away hair plastered across her forehead. She laid silently in his arms when the convulsions stopped. A distressed smile pushed through before she blacked back out. Her pants were soaked with her own blood and the muck he found her in. She looked as if she had been spit out of a beast.

Catatonic, Thyaz watched her for a long time. What rose up in him waiting to hear what her first words would be seeing him here blanked him. A huge bonfire threw grotesque shadows against slimy walls of a long, dark hall full of pulsing moans behind them. The dank,vaulted ceiling pressed the echoes down onto them all the more.

She sat up like a baby encased in something a mother would have to lick off, pulling at the gunk, disgusted. "Just like Plato said..." she spat.

Thyaz grunted, shocked after having waited so long for her to speak. She looked at him like she expected no one else. "What-?!"he hissed, bewildered.

"Plato…," she grumbled, confused at how she could be blushing at him here, now. Dead. Kinda. After life.
"What you think is reality is no more than shadows thrown against the only wall you let yourself see-" she stopped, uncomfortable with him looking at her for the first time in forever.

He took a sharp breath, digging his nails into his thighs to calm himself down, to pace what was on the tip of his bruised tongue. "You… just... died- and you're thinking about some other guy who died God only knows when-" he snarled,

"..Instead of who… HAD ANYTHING TO DO with you that happens to be right here?!-Plato?! Fucking Plato?!" he snapped, actually hurt.

"WHAT!?!" Artyo barked as she tried to lift herself out of his lap and discovered that her legs refused to move.

"What do you mean, What?!" he yelled, taken aback by her rage exploding when she'd been sleeping like a baby in his arms just moments ago.

"I literally killed myself so I wouldn't have to hear you harassing me in my head anymore!" she screamed.

"Bullshit! If you didn't want me to find you, why'd you wear the peryphs, Artyo?!" he snarled and flicked the bindi-like dots on her temples. He stood up, dumping her off of his lap. She gasped and angrily spat at him. Bloodied spittle hit his cheek."How in the hell can you spit that far but are unable to walk? Nope! Nevermind! I don't even care!" he growled then started off down the hallway, his legs heavy with the emotional weight of her.

"Good! Walk away! Leave! Where the fuck are you going to go to in here?! Take this motherfucker with you-" she yelled after him, pointing to her head. "Go ahead and leave, Thyaz! I won't follow this time either! Fuck you- don't believe me?!" she ranted. Thyaz focused on making his legs move, trying not to hear her. "Now you see how it feels-" she sobbed roughly.

He whirled around and screamed "How what feels?!"

"To have love-look you in the face as it denies you! That's what you did to me again and again, And look at you! After all that narcissistic bullshit-YOU couldn't live without Me! You fucking followed me here?! Why?!" Artyo screamed.

If she could walk right now, I'd so be gone! he thought to himself. He knew she was too weak to stand up and there was no way he'd leave her here, even if they had to drag each other by the hair to get out of wherever here was. *Yeah, and when she could walk,* another voice chimed in, *she'd hunt us down wherever this is and tear our skin off.* Imagining her doing it made him smirk.

"And what in the hell do you have on?!" she sneered.

"WHAaaat?!??!" he yelled at her in disbelief as he self consciously ran his hands over his tight black tee-shirt with cut-outs along the shoulder line.

"Lemme guess!Some Hostess on loan to you for servicing told you it showed off your wares? You fucking byshunfu!" she cackled ."You have the nerve to die in that?! After I worked my ass off on all that gear for you to take to Japan- a fucking trousseau- You die in This?!"

"You don't like what I have on?! Good! You get more pissed off over things you see versus the shit you should just know!! And you want to blame it on what I knew? You should have stayed your ass in New York and waited!! I told you what I was going to do-You should have waited! But you know everything, right?! Why didn't you know I'd come back?! You're not even angry about what went down the first few years! You never gave a fuck about anybody I had hovering near me! You had faith enough in me then! Or! Why couldn't you ask me to stay with you??! Then none of this would have happened, Artyo!" he yelled.

"I should have known to ask you to stay?! You're the one who dropped going back to Tokyo on me while I was organizing the fucking company you promised to come back and run With me- AND YOU HAVE THE GALL-The guy who screamed at me about pressuring him to stay the day I had to track him down to tell me the truth?" she screamed.

"You didn't even give me the chance to figure out what I wanted because the fucked pahpi you picked told you all women were as passively fucked as your mom on some fucking island in the mid seventies -Nope! Fuck that!! Won't even go there! -You didn't have the balls to figure out what you wanted- and you mosey your narrow ass into my afterlife! I should be rejoicing over you finally showing up After I died?! Fuck you!"

Thyaz snarled." Yeah, all This "you picked your father" shit coming from the bitch who just murdered every person in her fucking family- including her OWN fucked-up Handpicked pahpi- Don't you go anywhere near the topic of choice-"

"What? You thought you wouldn't be accountable here?" she laughed and then started to cry.
"I don't even know where the fuck I am! I didn't know here existed, Artyo!" Thyaz screamed.
"Which makes it worse! It means you really were trying to leave me! Even after-" she choked down tears and turned away from him.

"Look at me." he whispered, mollified, inching closer to her. She turned further away. "Look at me!" he barked. Artyo bared her teeth at him. "I -am sorry. Okay? I am SO sorry. But I'm Here! I'm "here" Artyo! If being here- Wherever the hell here is- together doesn't make it right- What am I supposed- What else do you want me to do?" he cried out softly.

Artyo shrugged her shoulders. Thyaz sighed and sat back down in the muck beside her for what felt like an eternity. Finally, she spoke."Why can't I stand up?" she whispered hoarsely.

"Cause your legs still think you're dead. They're shocked by the violence of how you left-" he replied. "Do you know where we are?" he asked.

"In the bowels of heaven I guess... have you seen anything else?" Artyo asked.

"The Bowels of Heaven? Why would Heaven- and why would we-" Thyaz started but she cut him off.

"Where do you think you go if you kill yourself?"
"Hell?" he declared, surprised.
"Where do you think we just left, ya frickin Episcopalian?"

Silence settled in again.
"Only spinning swords." Thyaz said. He knew she was about to ask again.

"Spinning swords?" she repeated and sat up a little straighter, eyes on fire.

"Yeah, passed about ten or so of them as I tracked your signal from your peryphs," he grinned and acted like he was going to flick her in the temple. "Wait- twelve. Why?"

"Do you know which direction you came from?" she asked excitedly.

"Come here-" He pulled her to him before she could snake out of his reach.

"Do you remember which way you came from?" she repeated as he yanked her wet vestyr over her head, systematically removing her gear until she was sitting in her undyrs.

"Of course I do- but- & I know- you and that "13" transcendence shit-can you walk yet?"

"No."

He self-consciously removed all of his own gear. "Stop looking at me like that," he grumbled as her eyes crawled across his skin. She continued to stare, left thumb stuck in her mouth casually, index finger crooked over her nose.

Layers came off and he just stood there, the half wasted away body of a god. "What did you do to you to get so skinny?" she whispered sadly.

"It doesn't matter anymore-" he said as he bent over, spat on his fingertips and daubed at the blood on her face. Artyo looked at him curiously for a moment then looked down. She whistled at the black latex trunks with serrated edges she'd made for him years ago. "You're invading my privacy-" he warned.

She turned shyly away. He blushed and pulled her up. They stood face to face for the first time in ages. Barefoot. Eye to eye. "I can't believe you died in them-" she whispered.

"Shut up" he blush-grinned then chuckled "Let's go," He pulled her forward to make her walk a few steps on her own.

"Carry me-" she ordered, albeit softly.
"I am not carrying you- you're as big as me!"
"You're like three inches taller when you stand up straight! And you weigh more-" she fussed.
"But Look how skinny I got!" he yelped.
"I can't walk! Besides, we might as well put those glorious shoulders of yours to use-"
"Artyo, I am not carrying you!" Thyaz yelped.
"Fine- then we wait-!"
"Why do- why do I have to wait-?!" he sputtered, trying not to laugh.
"If you don't, when I catch up to you, I'll-fn-kill you-" she snarled.

"Well Maybe a little bloodlust will make you walk sooner-" he grinned as she covered her own blush-grin and crumpled to the ground. "You have got to lose those coy Japanese schoolgirl mannerisms- they don't fit you," he whispered, looking down at her over the tip of his nose.

"You still don't get that mines weren't fake- your Japanese

schoolgirls were. But you will soon."
"Artyo-" Thyaz sighed, "what's the point of leaving hell behind if you keep talking about it?"

"...Carry me...." she said simply.

He sighed melodramatically and pulled her up off the ground again. "I'll walk slowly-"

chapter two

Every penthouse and hotel alley in Tokyo had been scoured for even the slightest imprint of the one called Thyaz. Days ran into weeks, to no avail.

"With the luxurious laps he was tending to and roosting in, this makes no sense." Khrystos muttered.

The crush of hungry Hostess bodies that usually was both suffocation and solace to his Denizen frame when on atmospheric AWOL now stabbed like splinters into his stomach as he sprawled on the plush banquet under them, rocked by the battalion of angelic monkeys on his back that goaded him to go out of the dark into the light to look for him again.

He groaned, shoved the clutch of claustrophobically cute chicks off of him into the Salarimen streaming in early for service with no idea how much of their salaries they'd already blown there that month, and pushed back out into the already muggy Roppongi afternoon.

Weary-eyed, Khrystos paused and counted his steps in reverse. Again. He knew something was wrong, even without their overbearing Denizen psychic press. A gaijin shoved past

Khrystos, spiritually reeking of things that would have had him jailed in a heartbeat if he'd been caught.

"Dude's kindred in these streets, obviously-" Khrystos muttered to himself as he struggled to light the Gauliose cigarettes he'd made a habit of smoking to blend in with the gaijin norms tooling around the pleasure sector.

He paused. The rude boy paused too. The hairs on Khrystos' neck stood up as if he'd been seen. AS. He looked over. Rude Boy turned just enough to let him know he wasn't imagining things and darted down an alley. Khrystos ran after him, ears pounding as he gave chase through the grimier edges of Roppongi where neither Nihongin nor Gaijin gave much of a fuck for appearances.

"Yo! STOP RUNNING, MAN!" Khrystos roared like the terrifying deity he technically was. The Rude Boy froze as he rolled up on him, panicked look in his wild eyes.

"What do you want from me, maaaan?!! I didn't do anything, maaaan!" Rude Boy started whinnying like an old san Francisco Deadhead as he curled up in a ball in the middle of the dead-end alley roughly wedged between three beaten-down shack entries attached to larger old buildings beyond, the oldest structures in the neighborhood that seemed to be allowed to molt down into nothing in the dank disarray around them.

"Then why did you run, ya dumb fuck!? Got me out here actually running-" Khrystos grunted. He followed Rude Boy's gaze as his eyes darted to a brick jutting out of a pile of garbage. "Motherfucker, I will End you for even thinking about that-wait what the fuck-?!"

Stunned, Khrystos stared into the broken window on his right at a filthy, pale bare foot he could see gleaming in the dark. Rude Boy popped up, bricked him and bolted like the skittish animal he was.

"I'm not going back to Cali, maaaan!" he screamed over his shoulder as Khrystos slammed into the rickety door that was all that stood between him and the Lost motherfucker that had been somehow found.

chapter three

The hall seemed to go on forever. They moved at a turtle's pace, like a hunched over old couple. Before long, Thyaz lifted her onto his back. They traveled in silence, indifferent to the groans from the shadows.

"Hey,"
"What?" Artyo answered.
"Still mad at me?" he grinned like a Cheshire cat.
"My Dad said that to me once.....once-" she laughed darkly.
"See!" he groaned, as sheepish that she still remembered his favorite line from Johnny Dangerously as she was by his using her father's favorite line.

When they couldn't walk anymore, they slept. Together. For the first time. Arm in arm, legs wrapped around each other like children who had never known sleep without one another. When they couldn't bear the weight of the ground any longer they got up and walked again. Her legs got stronger, but he seemed to like carrying her after all his fussing to the contrary. "...Penance." Thyaz grumbled.

The longer it took, the more they got to squash between them. The better it felt to forgive. "How long did it take you to find me?" she whispered more than once.
"You don't want to know-" Thyaz always answered.
"Makes me wonder how long we've been out of hell-" she laughed the last time he said it.
"Makes me feel like how long doesn't exist here-" he whispered

as she wrapped her arms tighter around his neck. He pulled her deeper into his chest, both of them drunk off of feeling each other's skin.

There were only paces and pockets of sleep. Pure incubation.

Thyaz woke to find her looking at him wrapped around her, grinning. "What?" he whispered.
"You wouldn't recognize yourself now..." Artyo replied, fingers pressed into his frame. He looked like the perfected being she had always seen him as, no matter how corrupt he was.

"You wouldn't recognize you, either..." he murmured into the flesh of her waist as he closed his eyes, drunk off of how iridescent she'd begun to glow and how calm her eyes had become.

"I guess that means our journey is almost over, desho?" she whispered back.
"After finally just beginning?"he paused. "I mean I guess so, if us making up is the actual point of all this," he laughed and pulled her on top of him. Thyaz nuzzled the space between her breasts, headed towards her mouth and kissed her back to sleep.

For an eternity he lifted her still sleeping body into his arms, carrying her backwards until she woke up. Something inside of both of them knew whatever this was would soon come to an end, and both of them wanted to make it last for as long as they could without disturbing the other with their thoughts of brevity. But suddenly, out of nowhere something pulled him forward instead of back.

She awoke to the jolt of his quickening pace. The atmosphere glowed red the closer they got to the end of the hall. When they arrived in front of the last oscillating blade, Artyo climbed off of him and took in the spectacle with an insane grin on her face.

Thyaz and Artyo stood between the guards and leaned back to take in the lush overgrowth that had sprung up around them since the memory of it all was seeded.

The sentinels ignored their presence. Anything that had gotten that far- which was not as rare as one would think-had always been deterred by the razor sharp knife cutting through the atmosphere between them. The fear of those who ran away had made the sentinels absently begin to believe in the power of the blade themselves.

They looked exactly like the picture of them in the Jehovah Witness book of Bible Stories for kids she had grown up with, down to the snarls chiseled into their stony skin. The grimaces she had gotten in trouble for pointing out so long ago still did not reach up to their eyes.

Artyo and Thyaz clasped hands, both seeing the spinning blade in front of them but not believing in it for different reasons. They looked at each other, kissed and threw themselves headlong through the hologram of the oscillating sword.

Even if the Cherubim had taken more interest in them ahead of time they would have reacted too late to stop themselves from being butchered by the blades that had made their job of standing guard so ridiculous in the past.

Chunks and sparks from metal smashing stone spewed into the hallway and the portal collapsed in on itself, almost barricading the end hall entirely.

chapter four

The detectives assigned to the original Jaymes case watched their worlds burn from the separate safe houses.

They'd been spirited away once all Hell broke loose when all else they'd been up to came to light. They snarled at the same time unknowingly, for utterly different reasons, due to the symbiotic, almost telepathy that comes with twenty years of working with a man who is as entrusted to you as you are to him.

"Animals- Fucking Stupid Animals!"

The cop assigned to suicide watch over Detective Sam Henderson Jones bristled as he awkwardly leaned against the door, trying to tune the ranting of Jones out. "Who the fuck- Who the fuck do they think they are? The fucking-" Detective Jones snarled at the flat screen.

"Kids?" the cop muttered.
"What?!" Jones snapped incredulously.
The cop sucked air through his teeth and rolled his eyes.
"Nothing, man-" he mumbled.

"No! No-" Jones roared like the rotten fuck of a bully he was. "Apparently," he got in the wiry cop's face, sizing him up with the piggish black eyes of an asshole whose time was over without him knowing it, "it *was* something or you wouldn't have opened that sphincter of a mouth to say shit in the first place-" Jones rose to shove the insubordinate blank-faced cop.

The cop's eyes flickered with contempt, throwing the detective off guard.

"Don't you-" the cop seethed, "even Think about fucking touching me, you fucking piece of shit-"

Jones stepped back,baffled.

"It's fucks like you getting the rest of us fucking Killed out here- you and your fucking inability to Do. Your. Fucking. Job-" the cop hissed. "You spoiled fuck, look outside! Do You actually think-" he pointed out the window at all the cops in riot gear circling the house, "Do you think this is happening because you're some...sort of hero?! Because you're just some...Good fucking Guy whose brothers in Blue are willing to die for him?" The detective's beady eyes darted to his Kevlar coated brethren.

"Leave it alone, man! He's so fucking self-absorbed he can't even smell the smoke-" another cop low on the rung drawled with his back pressed to the wall beyond the door.

"Oh! You too?" Jones snapped defensively. 'You're barely a cadet, you fucking little piss ant-" he yelled. The hunched over cop pulled himself up to the 6'6" he'd been and feared as since the age of twelve and ducked into the room menacingly. The color drained from Detective Jone's face.

The wiry cop held out an arm to stop Rahn. "Not yet. He needs to live to see this shit."

"What?! What- what do you mean "Not yet?!" Jones blustered, "What the fuck are you gonna try to-"

Rahn shoved Jones so violently that he flew backwards over the takeout covered coffee table and crunched roughly against the stained safe house couch. "Shut up," Rahn whispered softly. "Tell him, Len-" Len sighed.

"They found the other safe houses. All of'em. Those *stupid animals~* The fucking kids torching this fucking city because of the shit you and your partner did-"

"There's no proof we-" Jones huffed hotly as the TV flickering on mute drew his eyes, "no proof we did Any-" the shaken detective whispered.

"They got your partner about ten minutes ago, Sam-"

Len un-muted the broadcast as Jones's blood brother, his literal partner in crime blubbered hysterically at each photo of victims his captors held up.   For every nod yes he was lacerated. For every fake head shake no he was viciously slapped again and again until he admitted to it.

Detective Sam H. Jones, son of another Sam that had pledged allegiance to the blue line like his Uncle Sam before him, hiding his psychosis in plain sight, looked on in shock.

Suddenly his partner cried out, broken. "Sa-Sam- I'm-sorr-sorry-" The detective started screaming.

 "That one's not mine! No! No! It wasn't me! It was him! I'm not taking the-!" he panted, wildly grabbing the stack of photos with shaking hands. Erratically he slapped down face after face onto the desk. "No! Nope! Not that one, either! I didn't- It wasn't me! Not her either! Fuck this! Fuck this shit! I'm not taking the wrap for all this shit! This bitch was his! It was him- most of these fucking whores were him!" he howled.

A kid in a black hoodie ran up and punched Sam's partner in the face so hard that the kids holding the box-cutters gasped in shock as they dove out of the way. The detective huddled in a ball on the dirty floor, whimpering as he pressed his destroyed face against the stained pink and yellow striped wallpaper he had torn when he'd slammed into it. He started sobbing.

"Stop crying!" The boy raged as he rained punches down on the detective's head until the man choked down his cries, swallowing them the way many of their victims had been forced to do. The other kids all knew better than to stop the kid.

Sam gasped in horror at the photos of his victims stacked neatly in the foreground of the grisly scene. He flinched each time blood, tears or spittle from his partner splattered onto his kills. The kid spun around and ripped the last photograph Sam's partner had touched off the pile, the one he'd disparaged as a bitch and a whore.

"NOTABITCH!" The boy roared. "MY. Fucking. BEST. Friend! You fucking asshole! Her name was Chrystul! She was fourteen! FUCKING FOURTEEN! A violinist! Not a fucking Whore!" he cried, chest heaving as he tried to catch his breath. "Not a whore! No matter WHAT you two fucks made her do!" Trayvon screamed, then suddenly got terrifyingly calm.

"You're lucky I don't slit your fucking throat right now-" he growled.

A girl that couldn't have been more than 15 stepped in front of the camera with eyes that gleamed with the darkness she'd obviously already survived before Armageddon had even broken out.

"THIS-" she snarled, "is the hill you Police fucks wanna die on? This piece of shit is who you're choosing to serve and protect instead of us?! This guy?!" She looked over her shoulder, shook her head, then glared back at the camera as if she could see the cops in the room protecting Sam and was taking a head count. "This is the Blue Flag you fucks still wanna raise?! All for...SAM...sweet, sick....sonafabitch Sam-" she muttered, her eyes falling on where he was on the couch like she could see him.

"So Be It." Makaila muttered. She closed her eyes. The kids behind her froze, faces half hidden by masks as they turned towards her expectantly, eyes flashing like they could feel it coming. "Lets burn this bitch to the ground! Let's make sure they see this hill they're choosing to die on flaming from fucking Heaven!"

"Raise their fucking flag!" Trayvon yelled.
The kids went berserk.

Sam's partner screaming as the kids wrapped one of the ropes that he'd used on their victims around his neck was beamed out live before Makaila swung the camera away from the carnage to a close-up of her face as she walked.

"You know where we are-because we found him where you hid him," she purred, "you still have time, too. You can send whatever you got to snuff us out...but it's just going to alert the rest of us to ...where sweet old SAM ...is-" she laughed, "and then...we're gonna cut you down-" she paused. "Or..."

Makaila lifted the camera and walked down the hall filming Sam's partner as he was dragged up and out.

"Or you can wait for us to find what's left of you like the others-Or!" she laughed like the child she still technically was.

 Static and the newscaster's nervous voice boomed over the live feed. "We seem to be losing them-"

The screen filled with white as the camera adjusted to the pigeon shit gray sky above a destroyed neighborhood that had already been evacuated like the others due to the controlled burn of the kids across the city in search of the detectives. "We're back-" the newscaster whispered, rapt.

Makaila smiled sweetly into the camera in broad daylight. "Or you can match this stolen-no, Captured flag of yours-" she spun the camera to the front of the ramshackle two story house just as Sam's partner was violently pushed off the second floor porch and hung on national television.

The kids cheered as the Detective's body jerked around like a
fish out of water, just like all the young adults they'd lynched in
their rampage and got listed as suicides on their death certificates
to block insurance payouts to families that had been browbeaten
into taking out policies in the first place.

"With the blue flag you know we want to end this fucking shit."
she whispered. She trained the camera on herself again.

All those who'd covered their faces until that moment took off
their masks, glared balefully at the screen then scattered like the
wind behind Makaila. "We don't care about you seeing us
anymore. We're not the criminals here. You are," she growled.
Besides... if you see Any of us now, it'll be the last thing you
fucking see-"

The live feed went dead.

The anchor cleared her throat. "Well! There you have it!" She did
her best to hide the joy triggered by the visions of Peabody
awards dancing in her head and forced a somber tone to return to
her voice. A solemn look spread on her face as she summarized
the situation so far, fresh on the heels of possibly the first on-air
lynching of a cop to ever have been broadcast by her parent
company. Ratings Bonanza.

"The insanity that began with the grisly, generational massacre
of the parents of Artyo Jaymes and her clan of cousins, attacks
which catapulted decades of depravity festering beneath the
surface of the child-focused social and justice institutions here in
our beloved city of Cleveland onto the international stage rages
on. Even after the body of Ms. Jaymes was identified at the
scene of a suicide by cop-slash- triple homicide in Manhattan's
Central Park, the tsunami-like waves of copycat killer-slash-
abuse victicm vigilantes continues to slam the shores of every
echelon of our society."The woman inhaled greedily. "It is

unclear if the officers protecting Detective Samuel Henderson Jones were tuned in to hear that crudely specific list of, well..." she paused, "Demands, really-"

Len turned off the broadcast. Him and Rahn looked at one another as the rest of their brothers in blue pressed into the room.

"Fucking Fuck- Fuckin-" Jones stammered.
"Kids! Fucking KIDS!" Len yelled. " Sisters, Brothers! Cousins! Classmates! Same age as all the ones you and him slaughtered!"

Rahn moved out of dodge as Len charged Sam. "Say it with me! Kids! These fucking Kids!" Len screamed as he grabbed Sam by the face. "Fuck this! You're fuckin scum! I'm not dying for you!" His hands slid to Sam's throat.

"235 officers have been killed or wounded in this, Detective-" a superior they all knew called into the room before he entered.

The cluster of blue cops parted like the Red Sea as Lieutenant Barry Harris crossed the threshold. "Let him go, Len," he said softly. Len refused. Sam struggled away and climbed up the back of the couch, cagily pressing himself into the corner.

"As your superior, Sam… I watched those photographs that...he refused to cop to... pile up." He paused.
"The bullshit flimsy excuses you told me came back, too. Every single one, along with my looking the other way. " Lt. Harris muttered.

"Because that is... just what we do for each other, right? That is why we are All here, gentlemen." He looked at Sam. "Two hundred and thirty five other officers, Sam- But I don't blame you for any of their souls in this hell. I blame us all. We've all played blind."

Harris looked angrily up at the ceiling and sighed." I blame me for you, though." Sam looked stricken for the first time in all of this.

Harris spoke evenly. "Because there was a window. One that Jaymes kid flung open a long ways back. One I have never been able to forget. To this day, I have no idea how she even got forwarded to me. We have shit in place to block just that sort of thing from Ever happening... But SHE somehow was connected directly to the One person... Who could've stopped you from going after her big brother who you knew had also been attacked."

Sam tried to defend his actions but Harris rolled his eyes and angrily cut him off.

"You and your partner were fuckin' out of order! You were filling fuckin' quotas instead of doing the detective work you got promoted to do in the first place! All you had to do was find where the family had hidden the cunt attacking their own kids, you insolent Fuck! For Fucks Sake, Man!" Lieutenant Harris grimaced. "I should have done more than just tell you to back off her brother. Your rage at her blocking you from going after him through me was the real beginning of this shit-show with you two that we're all in now-"

Sam opened his mouth in protest but only spittle came out.

"You don't even remember, do you? Those kids who set off all this avenging angel shit...the ones who wiped out every adult in their family that you and him conspired with, and then went off and defiantly killed themselves before we could track them down like THEY were the villains and arrest them?!" Harris paused.

"Their faces aren't even IN that fucking pile! Their blood is on my hands, too." The Lieutenant pulled out his standard issue. "But your blood?...aw…your blood belongs to me."

Lieutenant Barry Harris shot Samuel Henderson Jones in the face at point blank range in front of everyone.

"You heard the kid. String his ass up. UP. Then go home to your families. If you can. And pray. That these kids are appeased."

"Lt. Harris, No!!!" Len screamed a second too late as Lieutenant Harris shot himself in the head and crumpled to the floor like a punctured paper bag.

"You heard the man's order." Rahn said coldly, picked up the limp body of his commander and carried him outside.

Len and the others grabbed the lifeless body of Detective Samuel Henderson Jones and dragged him out by his feet. By the time both bodies swung from the blooming branches of the cherry tree out front every nearby block was engulfed in flames.

Kids looked on from the ruins in shock at seeing the cops string the two up, finally moving in service of them, protecting them. The cops pulled off their Kevlar and knelt in the streets, not one feeling worthy of going home to families they'd never be able to look in the eyes again anyway, not after all that they'd sanctioned, done or swept under the rug.

The first child to walk up was a kid named Tamir. He locked eyes with a mealy-faced police officer and all the unnecessary violence the cop had ever committed against kids that looked like Tamir flashed between the two of them. The man broke down crying. More kids shuffled forward out of the smoke and clustered around the kneeling cops like priests delivering Last Rites. The officer heaved, shaken as he handed the butt of his gun to Tamir. The other cops followed suit, giving their guns to the smallest kids near them, who passed the firearms back through the crowd and awkwardly hugged the shattered males who'd destroyed communities due to never ever having felt like real men.

The smashed blue shield sobbed in the spindly arms of the multi-hued cluster of cherubic kids whose homes and neighborhoods the cops had made into a war zone to justify their reign of terror and weapons budget.

Makaila pushed through. With a flick of her chin the final safe house was engulfed in flames. She looked for the flag. "Who the-" she whistled, seeing the two bodies instead of one. " Ah~ You must be Sweet Sam's commanding officer-" Makaila whispered. "There's always one above signing off on the carnage below."

Slowly the small children were extracted and the camera spun up into the leaves.

"We're connected," the camerawoman hissed to her adrenaline soaked news anchors.

The cops shuffled to face up towards their slain comrades' soles together. One by one the cops placed their hands behind their heads.

"This is Sarah Jaipur, back with the latest developments in this breaking story-" the lead anchor sung out breezily as the cops were mowed down on live television, gangland style, closing demonic circles they'd opened in every community they'd infected in Hell on Earth.

chapter five

Khrystos cursed the dirty gaijin hippie as his body decimated the rickety low door to what had once been an old factory back entrance. He stood up, angry to see his own blood glinting like crushed rubies in the short, dark hall, then immediately became afraid. It was the first time he'd bled back on earth and didn't know what kind of alarms would be kicked off due to it on the Empyrean grid. He turned around, right into a big fist smashing into his jaw.

"The Fuck!" he roared and swung back on the beast that had nailed him in the face, tackling him in the dark before the other demons on the Yakuza pinned him there. "NO!!" Khrystos screamed as the densely packed dude the demons had ridden in on delivered the final blow to a barely conscious Thyaz.

The gangster flicked Thyaz's blood off his hand absently, rifled through his pockets and pulled out the vial of black stuff Thyaz had willfully stolen and held it up in the half-light. He stood up, dusted off his knees and walked right past Khrystos, obviously able to see him and ambivalent about it.

"You fucking yakuza- you think that's it? You're just gonna fucking murder him in broad daylight and walk the fuck away?!" Khrystos yelled, struggling against the demonic grips holding him that got stronger the angrier he became.

The gangster paused, a black silhouette in the white light pouring through the door frame from outside. "Kind of dark in here. Who saw me? You?" his chuckle slid into a snarl. "I know what you are- You're AWOL- You only halfway exist here. You're as Bakemono as them...just like me-"

"You fucking Yaju!" Khrystos roared like a beast himself. The gangster bristled at the insult. He turned and walked back to where the demons had Khrystos pinned to the dirty floor.

"Pick him up. Up. Not that high-" he muttered. The devils rammed Khrystos into the wall and held him so that he'd be awkwardly just below the sight-line of their boss.

"See… what you don't understand… is that I am neither."

"Not a monster. Not a murderer." The gangster got all the way down into the face of Khrystos. He scowled insanely but spoke eloquently, like a politician. " What YOU...Interrupted...was the culmination of a classic, suicide by theft."

He pulled out the black viscous filled cylinder, opened it and rammed it under the nose of Khrystos, who yanked his head back violently. "Ah yes~ You would know what this is, being what you are..." the gangster smirked and closed the vial.

"Very valuable here, more so than anywhere else, actually. I am NOT a monster!" he barked in the Denizen's face, then regained composure. "Just a gentleman, an Angel of Death, and Angel of Mercy, really- walking out the fulfillment of a Pointed request."

The gangster shook off the insult and walked back towards the exit. "And by the way? There is no sin in honoring a dead man's final request..." he called out, "especially when he made it while still standing up."

Khrystos cut everything he could about the gangster into his mind's eye, knowing they'd cross again. The yakuza dude flinched as if he felt the spiritual ping.

"Crack his case~" he murmured casually over his shoulder then walked off, wholly in cahoots with those who'd ridden the shell of him that was left like monkeys on his back for decades.

"Know your place, fucking Interloper-" the head demon snarled and threw him to the ground.

Khrystos lunged and knocked him the fuck out before being taken back down by his brethren who spiritually stomped him until he blacked out.

chapter six

Artyo saw nothing but red.
She blinked and blue skies returned where there had been white.
She outright rejected it.
Knew better.
Was not letting another reload chart the course she was to take.

Blood seeped across her sight-line, blotting out the crowd that had gathered around what had once been her body, a vehicle that had been desecrated early on, yet had still served her better possibly than she'd deserved.

She thanked her ship for its service as the sirens got nearer and closed her eyes as the metallic white sky of late summer in NYC returned behind the heads of the gawking and photo snapping joggers bearing witness to her demise in time for her final breath.

Her eyes popped back open, skin crawling as she stood on the doormat listening to him rant inside the house. The air was heavy with the ones assigned to keep him in the thick of it until he choked. A nervous titter danced across the outskirts of them as they recognized who and what she was.

They began to crowd around her, accusing her.
"You?! You dare to come here! You are the root of all evil!"
"Look to the left! Look at the house next door! Look at what you did, you self-righteous brat!" the demons who'd always been in cahoots with him brayed at her.

She glanced ambivalently towards the home to the left of the porch she stood on as it burned, perpetually engulfed in fire due to what he'd all but sanctioned to happen to all of them within it.

She smirked. The flames climbed higher in the green-tinged sky. The demons gnashed their teeth in horror, admonishing her.

After giving up on stalking his first wife while in bed with her replacement ten houses up the road, a woman who'd divorced him after torturing him for a matching set of eighteen years the first one had gotten out of him, he'd chosen to buy the house next door to the one he'd grown up in, the one all his kids had been sexually assaulted in by his youngest sibling, sans any intervention from him.

That move had been her first understanding that God was going to handle it His way, her initial comprehension that her father was going to go crazy due to it all, dead or alive. But she'd never expected crazy to look quite like this.

"You're not even supposed to BE here!"
"You're not even allowed here!"
"Hey! What are you doing?!"

The screams of demons in cahoots with the darkness of his heart got caught in their throats as she scanned the door to look for the always hidden in plain sight key. She slid her hand through the beautifully wrought iron gate he'd made for the door and grabbed the key dangling hip height on the hook he'd built into the bar, knowing he'd gauged it off of himself the way he'd taught her to do with the long limbs she'd gotten from him.

"What the- But how did you even know that was there!"
 "No!"
"See, I told you! She's known all along! She's the reason!"
"I told you! I TOLD YOU ALL SHE WAS HIS real JAILER!"

A dark smile spread across her face as she unlocked the gate, stepped in and pulled it shut behind her before the demons could flood in. She deftly slipped her hand back through the gate, locked it and snapped the key off as they slammed into it and shrieked. A confused gasp erupted as bewilderment spread though the spirits. She left the inner door open so they could hear her take him from them and walked in.

Sniffing in disgust at the dank smelling living room, she stepped past the overturned giant plant pots he'd soldered little plates of hand cut steel to like armor, yanked open curtains and threw open windows. Green light and sulfuric air cut into the space.

He came up behind her and sadistically grabbed the hair at the back of her head. "Who the fuck gave you permission to touch anything in my house?!"he snarled.

She roughly stepped on his foot and he collapsed all six foot three and 230 pounds of himself onto her as she hit him in the groin with her left elbow then elbowed him up off of her with her right. She spun and brutally sucker-punched him in the face with her left. He careened across the room into the wall, knocking all the upside down pictures he'd smeared with his own shit off of it. Hurt, he laughed hoarsely.

"I forgot about that evil assed left of yours-" He raised his hand to stop the vicious firstborn of his loins from beating the shit out of him for touching her hair, like he'd taught her to do to anyone who came for it after years of abusive attacks on it in the hands of her own mother that he rarely had tried to stop. He went to wipe at his nose and saw it was already slick with blood. He looked around in confusion, unable to see the gore at the back of her head from where he was. He waved it off and wiped her blood on his all white vacation ensemble before he delicately dabbed at his smashed nose. "What took you so long to come say Hi, Bayh?" he chuckled.

She stepped forward.

"Everybody look out! She's got a gun!" he yelled and jumped away, laughing nervously as she bent down and picked up one of the fallen picture frames, initially not taking an eye off of him. She took in the dried mess he'd crossed her and her brother out of his distorted memories with, smashed the frame and pulled the pristine photograph taken by her aunt out from under from his literal shit. She threw the glass into the detritus and dirt that spilled out from the corners of the room.

He watched her solemnly as she pulled out a switchblade and cut her and her brother out of the photo. She crumpled the rest of the image and tossed it behind her."Oh! It's a knife!?"he snarked sarcastically. "I always thought it was gonna be a gun-"

"It was a gun, remember?" she said ambivalently. "I already shot your ass. And all your brothers and sisters after you. You don't remember? Alzheimers? Nah. I prayed to God you'd never forget any of that ...and you know better than most that my word doesn't return to me void-"

"Fuck you-" her father snarled.
"Already kinda did that too, didn't you, daddy?" she laughed.
 "I never touched you!" he roared.
 She continued as if he'd said nothing. "So it can't be Alzheimers. Maybe it's where the bullet got lodged. They probably didn't dig it out when they found y'all- When I led them purposefully to y'all- I mean, why bother? Another Black man with a bullet in his head, right? Just like ya daddy, right?"

"FUCK You, you little-" he hissed.
"Like I said, Dad," she splayed his snarl across her face for effect. "YOU...already Fucked me-"

"I SAID I never touched you!" he roared defensively.

"Nope! Three hugs! Whole life! Don't worry! I remember that shit too! But you fucked me all the same by what you let happen to me and what you did to ME after finding out. instead of to the one who'd-" she roared and then caught herself.

"But that's neither here nor there, is it, Flip? I mean, it's certainly not ...here," she said evenly. She looked around the room and motioned over to the table full of rotting food. "Sit down-"she muttered.

"Nah! Not turning my back on your Angelic ass! I'll fucking stand for whatever you think this is about to be-" he fussed.

The Wrath of Artyo grabbed her father by the face and shoved all 194 centimeters of him violently towards the dining room table. He tried to grab her back but his hands came away slick with blood as he stumbled towards it against his will, catching himself on the back rung of a chair. He angrily sat down.

She sauntered behind him. "You and your fucking angelic dress whites!" she laughed. "Only you'd look at this as a motherfucking vacation-"

"Oh, like we weren't already in hell." he growled.
She looked at the food and chuckled. 'Eat up."
He narrowed his eyes "So you can poison US again?"

"Number one, I didn't poison your ass, I shot you in the fucking head, like your moms shot your father in the head, but for different reasons. Keep it straight, old man!" she laughed.

"And too, there is no US here! Your ass is the only one in here! Nobody made that food but you!"

He glowered at her as the truth registered.

"Ah fuck… so you DO get that in the end your generation basically poisoned themselves enabling that beast instead of murking the monster who made her when you had the chance-Wow! And here I thought time wasn't working on you-"

He looked away in search of a vitriolic comeback. "What "you thought?" he jeered. "Only thoughts you have ever had worth a damn were mines! Even ya stupid momma could see that! No thought of yours was worth a damn! Who the fuck gives a fuck about you or what you think beyond the thoughts I gave you? I'm the only coherence your impressionable ass ever had! You are nothing but a walking thought of mines!"

"Then apparently your old, evil ass is suicidal, Flip-" she said plainly.

All the air sucked out of the room. Blood began to flow profusely down from the back of the Wrath of Artyo's head. "You know why I'm here more than I do, don't you?" she asked. Her father nodded woodenly. She looked around at the hell he'd fashioned for himself.

"This isn't going to work." she whispered.
"Yes it will."
"No matter how many hells you build," the Wrath of Artyo murmured, "she's never going to come and bust you out of them to put you out of your selfish, narcissistic misery. Me, here, now? Pissed that I had to pause my shit to deliver this bon mot to your stubborn ass? This is the closest you're going to get to that. This ONE time-"

"Bullshit. I know my daughter," her father groused.

"The part of her that would bash through all heavens and hells just to beat your ass for the lies you told on her and her brother didn't die fixated on you. She died keyed into a greater fucked up love than yours, one that had fuck all to do with you, that was the only thing that stopped her from killing you that summer she pressed charges in the first place. The motherfucker who stayed her hand, told her you weren't worth her throwing her life away by taking yours. Her craziness with him after that made her leapfrog past this part you groomed her to play-"

He reached under the chair and pulled a gun on the Wrath of Artyo. "Where the fuck is my actual fucking daughter,then?! Tell me before I put a bullet in YOUR head, you fucking Demon!" he shrieked.

"It's a little late for that,"she snarked as he emptied the clip on her face point blank. She opened her mouth. The bullets slammed in and out of the already destroyed back of her head and boomeranged into his groin as her body caved in on itself.

Her father bled out beside the shell of the Wrath of Artyo and watched as the makeshift hell he'd fashioned for himself to escape judgment crumbled. His body fought against the gravitational pull of the black hole where she'd been to no avail. He fell into the abyss that remained.

He came to on a patch of grass in a barren field, curled up in the fetal position, staring up at the fiery inferno of the home his cruel father had almost killed himself trying to provide. Now the house burned for reasons wholly different than it did for the Wrath of Artyo. This fire shimmered with the fuel of his own feces, beckoning him. In. To deal with it. Finally. All of it.

He hunched over, imagining the pain he deserved for what he'd done crackling across his back from blows that never came. He grimaced, stood up angrily in the silence, then started ranting again. There was no one there to slander or gossip to but himself. He held off for as long as he could before his nails sunk in and he clawed against the barely healed flesh pulled across his back himself. He spewed vitriol over his shoulder as he limped away from the homestead, away the only direction his mind could grasp.

A jolt of pain folded him back down, choking on the venom he trafficked in life after life, death after death.

chapter seven

Emancipation.
Burning hot.
The smell of seared skin.
Sound of static electricity.
Eyes closed.
Overwhelmed by the impossibility of darkness.

Afraid of not having eyes anymore.
Of not Being any longer.
Wanting to look more than life.
Choking on panic.
Grasping where fingers and hands were last.
Praying and groping in the darkness of the most vicious white.

Sudden crashing of flesh into flesh.
Eyes ripped open in relief.
Cowering together in shock.
Focused on each others eyes.
Not daring to look at anything but-
Nails dug into arms.
Not daring to blink in thin, harsh air.

Mountains of refuse slowly crumbling into rocky
desert that faded into white nothingness.

Artyo's jaw dropped open, a red sky reflected back to him in her
eyes. "WHAT The-?!" she screamed soundlessly.

Thyaz peeked around her hair that was suspended, as if she was
gliding downward. Red skies forgotten, he raised his left hand to
touch it. He drew back as the strands darted away from him like
they were alive. "...Art yo-your hair-"

"We're in-" Artyo started to stammer as she took in red as far as the eye could see.

"Artyo-check out your hair-" Thyaz repeated internally, entranced by the way her mane twirled in front of him. A cluster of hair dancing across her face stopped her short. She whipped around, Thyaz ducking out of the way as her mane oscillated around them, various lengths spinning in different directions at the same time.

"Coooool-" they whispered together, jumping a little at the sounds of each other's voices coming through externally for the first time.

"Wait-we're on steps-" Thyaz shouted as he looked below the two of them at the wide gold splashed staircase that seemed to tumble down into forever, disappearing into the white mists of clouds that slashed across the bright red sky. Artyo dug her fingers deeper into his flesh as the height registered, hurting him.

They looked up at a gold splashed outcrop rising above the highest of the stairs they could see. Artyo took off, hovering close to the stairs as she made a mad dash for what had to be a building resting up top.

Thyaz screamed after her, terrified. Slowly crawling upward, he cursed the day she died, almost blacking out from the fear of being left on the barren, glistening stairs to die, again, eyes closed to the red glare of the sky. She came back and dragged him up the stairs, her eyes shiny with tears. "I think I know where we are, but we can't be- but if we are where I think we are, we-" she rambled.

A terrace bent in at the top of the stairs, leaving the two of them on their knees in front of a giant carved head of an angry faced man drenched in gold, cracked from the impact of having landed there on its side. Behind the head a large complex climbed along a mountain. Gold rained from the gutters of bridge after bridge above them between the respective buildings. Directly in front of them stood giant slabs forty feet high, carved full of men the size of small houses with curly long beards and hair, skirts fashioned to look like the scales of fish and feathers, with wings angling off of their topless bodies. They waved date palms in the direction of an opening between the slabs that must have been used as the main entry where rivulets of gold poured down continuously from spigots above into grates on the ground.

Artyo ran her hands over the stone slabs, enraptured. The damp gold came off on her fingertips. Thyaz walked along the edge of the terrace, looking up at the mountain the place seemed to be suspended from. The thin air around them got hotter the longer Artyo stood caressing the bas-reliefs. Her skin, more sun burnt.

Thyaz crouched down and ran his fingers through the coppery sand that covered the terrace. His and her skin were coated with the dust, and although it stood out on him it seemed to be melting into her. It began to move across the surface of his skin as if the dust felt his eyes looking at it, then seeped into him too as he watched in shock. "Artyo-" he called over to her as he stood up and attempted to dust the sand off of his exposed skin. "Mahmi, I think we better go inside-"

"What's wrong?" she whispered and floated over to him as if in a dream, her hair billowing out behind her. He lightly grasped her wrist and turned it over so that the coppery flakes could be seen against it as they liquefied, soaking into her skin.

"I just think it would be better if we went inside of whatever this is-" he said softly, pulling her across the terrace to the opening of the main building. They stood in front of it for a moment, enjoying the silence, wondering if anyone or anything else was around on the other side of the cascade.

"What if this is a hologram like the sword?' she asked softly, her hair caught up in breezes they couldn't feel against their darkened skin but could see whipping up tiny cyclones of dust around their feet.

"Well, what did you believe you were going to see before we leaped through that?" he whispered.
"Where I came to first-" she paused, "Um...what did you believe we'd see?" Artyo peered up at where the rain of gold showered down from. He thought for a moment.

"...An explanation, I guess, for the both of us-"

She felt him smile before she looked over at him, knowing what needed answering immediately. Without thinking, he quickly kissed her.

"For luck,"he shrugged hotly and shushed any phony protests he was about to hear. They closed their eyes and on the count of three, jumped.

chapter eight

Khrystos came back to with a start. He grabbed his head and winced as flashbacks from the brawl whirled disjointedly inside his head before he opened his eyes.

The first thing he saw was the barefoot corpse of Thyaz beyond his toes, sprawled shoe-less at its center under a dirty, old skylight. The only other light came from the door he'd careened through and slashes that cut through the dank air from broken, papered over second story windows Khrystos was surprised to see the space had.

He lumbered over to him and couldn't tell if they'd beaten him out of his spiritual armour or if he'd stepped out of his peace shod shoes on purpose, trying to speed up the transaction it was now obvious he'd gone into fully cognizant.

The glyphed hairs on Khrystos's head stood up as he walked around Thyaz's broken body in a circle. His own blood he'd awakened in slid down his back and mixed with Thyaz's spilled blood as he went, amplifying it. A protective shield popped up around the body, signaling the Heralds.

"You fackin' idiot, man!!" Khrystos yelled. "You had Everything you needed here! You had the whole of Heaven rooting for you and yet still – THIS?! This is how you literally decide to go out?! Because of pride?! Being a "man"?! Fuck!"

The more time he spent in the company of the body of Thyaz waiting for it's BA & Ka to be retrieved, the angrier he got.

"She… was so fucking stupid when it came to you...but you know what? We were too. We ALL were- We had faith in you watching Her have it- and She couldn't be wrong, right?" Khrystos lit another Gauliose, took a deep drag and ashed next to the body of Thyaz. "But now, not only is *she* God only knows where after what and HOW she- Now you're fucking dead too?! And here?! In this fucking hovel?!"

The Rage of Khrystos flared up "And I end up getting jumped by smelly-assed demons, even? maan-All I fucking wanna do is stomp the life outta you for making my ass be the one who had to find you! If you weren't already dead I'd probably fucking kill you my damned-"

Khrystos froze mid rant as pressure in the space shifted.

Smelling legality in the air, he dropped the bent cigarette to the dusty floor and ground his combat boot into it. Narrowing his eyes, Khrystos slid into the shadows of the ramshackle building at the thud of ANC boots on the four points of the roof, fully Empyrean outfitted.

chapter nine

Sigrid's It Gets Dark punctuated the spaces between promised land streams ambling aimlessly on barely watched viewfinders levitating next to the shoulders of bored, obscenely perfected Denizens.

They penned themselves into the D/o complex with no place to go that made sense of how awkwardly they glowed out in the reddish realms's so-called light. They gleamed as they guzzled Heavenly brand tonic water that hit their quicksilver adverse systems the way cheap champagne hit the empty stomachs of lightweights down in Hell on Earth. It was a dirty high that kind of burned, but a dirty Denizen high in the dark to equilib them among kin was the only lean on offer.

It seeded them with a sloppy, defiant sense of solidarity that carried them as they glared balefully at the perfection they'd for some unknown reason been cast violently into. Watching their natural phosphorescence amplify and spread across the collective surface of themselves to sighs of relaxation and relief was the only semblance of peace they had where they'd found themselves strung up like lights. The off-key glow was how they found one another out in the wilds of 'what a wonderful world' afoot beyond the confines of the Demi-Ourgos theater. It was how they knew on sight who to nudge among the newly arrived and surely already disparaged by Citizens as Denizens to the place where the caginess woven onto their Kind could be allowed to wear thin for a while, where they could feel a sense of release.

An Otaku keyed to the order of the Holy Idiot sighed. "...I miss him~"
"I miss his goofy ass, too." another Tengu cried out softly.
"Me too! I know! Let's... Call him up!"
The clutch of Tenshi eternally tiger-beating for the one called Thyaz squealed.

"Whaat?!No! Not again!" a nearby Denizen yowled in mock disgust. "Come on yall! We watch yalls doofy dude allatime!"

More Denizens around the otaku cluster whined to no avail. "We rhove him and we miss him!!!" the teenybopper bodied Tenshi roared like Tengu, in unison.

"Nah! Look- those lil Tengu are spiritual bullies! Ioncare how innocent they vibrate out!" A perpetually disgruntled Denizen barked.
"We misss him! We haven't peeked in for eons~" The Otakus warbled melodically.
"Yall, we actually ain't checked in on his crazy arse inna-"
"Don't join in with them! Maan!" Pyntagon squeaked.

"F ureaking theatrics! Come on! We watch yall's guy All the time!" another pocket of Denizens further afield yelled with contempt as the idea wafted through the zone collecting votes.

"It's been FOR Ever!"
"Yall are addicted! They're addicted, I tell ya!" the one called Anzak chortled to his crew of angels sprawled across more stadium seats than needed as usual.
"Well, technically what the frick else are we supposed to do? What else do we all agree on in this never-ending pretty much inert state?" Newton shrugged.

The Denizens groaned as they were begrudgingly herded to come on one accord within the D/o theater by the cadres of Thyaz acolytes working the complex like go-go dancers doing what was needed to make an uptight night pop off.

The collective D/o stream began to jump back and forth through the simultaneous feeds in play until a majority consensus was reached and strands of his theme music began to pulse in the dark around them behind everything else they were patched into below.

The ones who'd fussed the most swayed harder in their seats to the bass creeping up than the Otakus in their sky high shoes already prancing around, hyping their brethren to their favorite lead-in rhythm until the entire complex pulsed with the vibration that kept them perpetually geeked.

The guitar riff from the intro to the theme music of Thyaz exploded from the core of the Demi-Ourgos complex. The feed spun out of control until it landed on Thyaz's gorgeously grinning face in his intro montage, big as a MAC truck beaming out of the fount of clouds. All the Denizens went wild cheering on their favorite idiot as high hats rung out and all of the Denizen class of Empyrean Angelic beings present within the space began dancing in the aisles.

The track scratched.

"What tha heck-oh my-" an Angelic being hissed.

The layers of the feed discombobulated as it unfurled and played like an old-timey film whose negatives had slightly disengaged from their tracking teeth.

"Where the heck did yall leave off on in his arc anyway?!"
"- Oh no-"
"Oh my-god-" The Otakus gasped in horror.

"Nothing keyed to that had anything to do with-"

Dried Blood. And excrement. Filth. Everywhere. Filth spilled out of the shadows, a room that obviously had been filthy long before its atmosphere was rife with the permeating smell of death.

"What is this?! How are we even seeing this?!"a bewildered Denizen yelled. "We can't see this! We CAN'T -there's no way to-" the Angel screamed again and again until he was hoarse.

The one called Khrystos surreptitiously slid into the space and shook his head woefully.

"Fuck, man! Fuuck!" Khrystos roared. The hairs on the back of his neck stood up as the atmosphere shifted even more. He spirited himself away into the darkness.

"What the-" a Denizen yelped.
"Khrystos?! Who has been riding Khrystos to get this kind of-"

The Thyaz Tengu within the D/o theater dropped to their knees like bricks off a building at the sight of their dead Saint.

chapter ten

Lamenters in Episcopalian garb portaled in, glinting in the dusty half light of the old factory as they morosely danced around the corpse of Thyaz. They sobbed, bereft at having to witness him in this state.

The Comptrollers had done everything they could to ensure that the corpse they swanned around had ended up no place but exactly where he was, dead on a dirty floor in a rubble filled room. They worked themselves up into a fevered pitch, elated to finally drag this shell where they'd made sure it would indeed belong, no gain of entry loopholes needed.

"He had so much more to offer life!" one wailed dramatically to the Comptrolling missionaries helming the retrieval. They nodded sullenly and flung themselves into the muck and mire surrounding the body.

"Dare I say it, but the warm...mist of life is still on him-" one whispered.

His brother froze. The mask of sadness he wore sat garishly askew on his face as other emotions and inclinations rose to the surface of him. He took another look at the felled man. "Ahh, yes- it does seem...the rigor-mortis has ...not yet ...set in-"

"Oh?" a missionary in nothing but a stained rochet piqued, his tongue suddenly thick with perverse lust. A foreboding smile spread across his cheeks until even the folds of fat at the back of his neck were flush with aroused blood in the dark. " Well in that case...then perhaps, my brothers...we should all have some … fun...while he's still... pliable...before dragging him deeper into H.O.E. to reload him-"

"Break this bread however you see fit, but make a fast show of it, for goodness sake-"a high-ranking elder in a cossack who'd gotten his fill long ago barked impatiently.

Another filthy missionary in just a surplice and a partially unraveled girdle hissed contrarily as he used his crozier to slide up the top Thyaz had chosen to die in as his fellow missionaries cavorted around him, drunk off the last vestiges of life that misted off of his newly exposed skin.

Body drenched in his own sweat, another missionary in the rochet dropped to his knees. The wet muslin suctioned to him as he crawled towards Thyaz's body, hand outstretched alongside his brother's crozier. but somehow unable to touch him, try as he may. Out of nowhere, incomprehensible chanting began to bloom in the space around the comptrolling Missionaries.

"What kind of darkness is this?!" he snapped, outraged by both the block and the purity embedded in the sound.

Comptrolling Monks coated in white like mourning Butoh dancers under their robes materialized with the casting of a cloud of ashes all over the shoe-less body of Thyaz as they tossed sacred water across it.

"Yogosanai-tai!"

The combination of their ashes and holy water made the Denizen demarcation of Khrystos pop up faintly but before the monks could even address it the offended Missionaries roared with displeasure at their rightful claim to pound the flesh being contested before it picked up speed by the light of their presence.

"What?! What is-"
"Do not contaminate- The Body!"
"How dare you judge our holy rituals as Contamination!" the elder Missionary in the cossack roared.

The missionary in the stained rochet demurred, "We are simply here to mourn and peaceably transport our lowly brother to his rightful next station, as is the norm with gaijins in the-"

"We know how you monsters mourn-" snarled Ire, a monk with a clean shaven head painted white except for his wild black brows, "over anything ...pliant."

"What are you Bozu daring to accuse us of on this hallowed ground?" the crozier wielding missionary barked.

"Of what we just literally interrupted you starting to do-" grinned a monk called Teru-teru because of sun that seemed housed in his mouth, even when his teeth were blacked out for processions.

"We've seen how you worship… and have had to... pick up the pieces of...bread you've left behind all over this zone- for what feels like an eternity. Not this time. Not this one."

"Who are you to tell us?! Our God the Lord doesn't bow to your Amitaba!"

 The Episcopalians exploded on the Comptrolling monks and tried to press towards the body to no avail. "Release him from whatever animistic sorcery you have wrapped around him! He was raised in our church! He's one of ours! Was even an altar boy!"

"No wonder you all are so aroused-" Teru teru smirked as his fellow Monks threw more ashes on the body defiantly, disgusted with the priests panting to defile the dead man even in full view of them. They shamelessly, lustfully lunged for the corpse of Thyaz.

"Your claim is voided by his gaijin life. He has made his home in Buddhist territory, spoke fluent Japanese, and has spent more time fornicating on the grounds of Buddhist temples in his time here than he ever spent at church as an adult- He is not of your flock, anymore than we are of yours," Ire growled.

"Retrieve what you want," the cossacked priest roared, agitated by the religious tit for tat.

"You can NOT touch the body until rigor-mortis sets in or he will remain trapped between bardos-" one of the monks sighed.

"HIM?Bardo-? He doesn't get the Option of your heathenish Bardos!Who knows what his Last thought was?!The life he's led makes him rightfully our parcel! To mete out whatever we wish to!" The elder Missionary raged.

"He was killed in our territory! Last words determine Last Rites!"

Two monks stepped toward his body with shakujo staffs. Two more muscled monks menacingly stepped forward and made the offended priests step back. One of the monks pressed his staff roughly into Thyaz's forehead as the other slammed his staff into his stomach to push the air in it up and out. His tongue stuck out with his last exhale, the kanji for I'm sorry roughly cut into its flesh.

"Ahha! Gomenasai!"

"If you think we're honoring that you're out of your Amitaba loving minds!"screamed the rochet draped priest as he lunged at a monk who pivoted down into horse stance and threw ash in his eyes. The priest screamed holy murder as a brawl broke out between the two religious camps.

"Enough of this shit-" Khrystos muttered in the shadows and sprung out into the opening between the corpse and the Comptrolling missionaries and monks.

Both religious gangs gasped and backed away from the Terrifying Deity that Khrystos read to them as on this plane.

"Fuck is wrong with you?" he hissed with disgust as he stepped towards a man of the cloth in nothing but a mitre. "You're that hungry for it afterlife? The draw of an empty vessel to...fill one last time is truly that strong that- even now, even knowing on sight that I can spiritually rip you in two... you're still standing here salivating, licking your lips, looking for your window of opportunity? Willing to risk it all for a little necro-"

The priest lunged past Khrystos towards the corpse of Thyaz like a punch drunk lover before he was yanked up in the air and dropped like a sack of potatoes onto the filthy floor. Shuddering death throes erupted across the surface of his body as all dark light within him was snuffed out.

chapter eleven

The priest awoke in a deep indent on a beach. He hoisted himself out. The open fish mouth hat and tattered habit shifted as he stumbled along the sand.

Bruised and battered, he called on the most high to not forsake him, to look at all the good deeds he did serving his god. Not watching where he stepped he tripped over an old bottle.

"A sign! Thank you, God!" He picked it up and saw a slip of paper in the corroded bottle. A message.

He hunched over, broke the bottle and unrolled it, oblivious to his fish mouth cap falling off as he did.

"even the sparrows must eat."

Mystified, he repeated it. Called, the carrion swarm came.

Talons and beaks slammed into his exposed skull with such force that every scream that tried to erupt out of his chest got stuck in his throat. His eyes rolled back in his head as he willed himself to pass out to no avail.

He felt the tiny tears in his flesh like little pieces of tape being pressed into him and pulled off, but knew it was his skin. The pain wasn't debilitating, it was the thoughts, the incessant thoughts. Thoughts that would both be the death of him and bring him back to life again and again.

Curling up in a ball exposed the back of his skull and it was as if he was somehow looking through his own brain and was able to see the small cloud of sparrows slick with what he knew was his blood at his nape as they dug in with their perfectly curved beaks, ripping his hair out at the roots in clumps.

"God! Why are you forsaking your chosen viceroy! I have served honorably in your stead always!"

His screams rung out. He sounded metallic, artificial, false. Every one of his own protests registered to his ears as so fake that silence clamped down violently between each gasp he took to fight off the truth. He retched and the rancid aftertaste of every innocent he'd molested and consumed the light of bloomed in his mouth as the stolen spirits pummeled his insides, clawing their way out of him, yanking him spread eagle, face down, like he'd left them all, defiled.

The cloud of carrion exploded up in the sky as he flopped over and screamed against the exodus of light leaving the pit of hell he'd built up within pockets of his soul. Pink Floyd Echoes whirled around them as they rose. The further up their flapping went into the sky the quieter it got around his prone body.

The spirits of his weakest victims seeped out of him, some not looking back, others looking over their shoulders with shocked grins, plastered with joy over the mangling of him that set them free.

Feeling the weight of the hole in his soul he'd crammed full of their innocence to not process the obliteration of his own, he actually began to cry. The truth slammed into him like an anvil.

"I have no right-" he whispered, spastic as it hit he'd been pitying himself, crying out for mercy without any remorse for what he'd consistently done, even as he was pecked to death by devouring little birds. Again.

No tuft of hair ripped out of him was ever going to be enough. Nothing he'd done would ever be rescinded. No pity would ever be delivered because none was due. He didn't deserve pity or pain. Only realization. That he didn't care whom or how many children he had destroyed.

In that moment he knew it didn't matter how many times he died here. Or what manner of cloth this man of God draped himself in as he materialized here. He'd be reborn again and again until he faced what he had done with his life. For what it was. Until he really understood with every speck of flesh upon him the monster he had chosen to become.

The first honest wail in his after-existence erupted out of him.

The carrion birds of every shape and size hammered down through the bruised, red sky towards him at breakneck speed, a streak of black lightning that hit his body with such force that his corpse was rammed deep into the ground as the feathered swarm devoured him, picking his bones clean as his soul screamed with his last breath and then blacked out.

"I deserve it!"

...A Baptist pastor awoke in a deep indent on a scarred beach.

chapter twelve

The Ulteriors Apoc, Apogee and Apex materialized in the alley outside the factory and looked up.

Crows slid through the thick atmosphere above the helmeted heads of the four Heralds that stood on the four points of the roof, looking down into the retrieval madness with disgust. Apoc and company portaled up onto the roof, sauntered over to the Heralds casually and started chatting. The black carrion swam in circles above the cluster of beings, smelling the death in the air.

"The pedales at it again?" Apoc grinned malevolently. The Heralds said nothing.
"And being somehow...thwarted, sounds like. Scebe, desho?" Apex chuckled.

The Herald nearest to him smirked. "We know whose Ulteriors you are- Cargo in house keyed to any of you rogues?"the Herald asked pointedly.

Apex sized her up. "On the record?" She raised a brow. "No," he whispered, "but-"

Apoc cut him off and addressed the lead Herald. "We can handle the whathaveyous at hand, off the books pretty quickly-"

Apex growled "We know how your kind loathes time in this atmosphere-"

"Could yall?The stench of this place just-ugh!" the youngest Herald started to fuss. She was silenced by Amybalis holding up her hand. The Heralds hands all go to their curved swords.

"Oh, for fucks sake!" Apogee howled, slammed her face shield down, passcoded the closest Herald in and leaped into the factory. Apoc & Apex gagged as the factory went silent.

Amybalis chuckled in Apoc's face, hand on blade. "Never been known for patience, that one- Do what it is that you do, Ulteriors-" Amybalis whispered and passcoded the stragglers into the fray after their unofficial Leader as the crows circled hungrily overhead.

chapter thirteen

Apogee landed barefoot next to Thyaz's head, shaking the foundations of the building.

The Monks and Missionaries looked up from their squabbling and screaming at Khrystos with a start. Apex and Apoc slammed down into the zone a few beats behind her. The atmospheric blast caused by their triple penetration of space roughly threw Khrystos into a wet wall and completely knocked him out.

Both the Monks and the Missionaries scattered. The Episcopalian Missionaries barely took a breath before they began yelling things out into the light at the interlopers from the shadows, cowering in the filth along the outskirts of the half-lit space.

They shielded their eyes from surely what had to be Angels of a God they claimed to serve in name no matter the actuality of their deeds, but ranted in outrage all the same, the Comptroller psychoses keyed to Manifest Destiny unable to allow them the forethought of subjugation to anything, even when it obviously spiritually outranked them.

"Wait!-What in the-"
"What's happening!?"
"What IS this? Who- What are you?!"
"What gives YOU the right to intrude on our assigned protocols, whatever you deign to be?"
"Who do you three spiritually report to?!"

"Is this Comptrolling motherfucker low key asking to speak to our manager?" Apogee grunted, stunned.

"Is there anything low key about the braying of these necrophiliacal spiritual dustpans?"a bemused Apoc muttered.

"These pedales all sound pretty high key to me..."Apex shrugged, "since they're ringing a bell, perhaps we should-"
 Sonafa! Apogee-" Apex groaned as his violent Sister-in-Arms grabbed a rochet robed Missionary by the throat and ripped him up into the air.

"Who do we report to?" Apogee hissed up at the man of the cloth, "Someone your screams couldn't reach even if you tried due to all the sick shit you've done doing your job, but here- let me help you try to hit that pitch all the same-" She squeezed his neck so hard that his vocal cords burst in his throat.

His brothers screamed, horrified. Blood danced down her forearm before it dripped onto the floor and pooled directly beneath her elbow. A sweet smile splayed maniacally across her face under her mask. Apogee stepped into the spiritual blood of the rochet wearing Comptroller and wriggled her toes like a child to the revulsion of his brethren.

Apoc whistled.
"Not even a- and oMG! You're- That's the first time your ass has smiled in eons!" Apex crowed sarcastically.
"She does look, dare I say it? Happy, right?" Apoc chuckled.
"Mayhem, unnecessary may...hem!" Apex laughed.

"

The correct pronunciation is Ma'am~!" Apogee growled.
"That is not the word I was trying to Say, Ms. Apogee!" Apex chuckled as the bleating of the Missionaries got louder. Apogee scowled at their displeasure, violently flung his broken body at their feet and stepped back over to the crown of Thyaz's head.

Cut from a different cloth altogether, the terrified Monks looked on, mollified and demoralized.
"Yamantaka,desu-ka?" Teru-teru hoarsely whispered to Ire.
Ire stood beside him, as scared as all the other monks in their retrieval party.
"Mahakala?" Gozen choked.
"Iie," Ire shuddered. " Servant Warriors? To be sure… but whatever this is at play is clearly beyond anything we've been told Mahakala deals with in this realm-"

"What has this parcel of flesh done to draw so much-"
"Are we to dishonor ourselves and defile our sect by mingling with such a press?"
"From the looks of them, nothing would be left of our sect if we did have the unmitigated audacity to-"
"Not our bucket of monkeys at all!" Gozen muttered. His hand rammed into his pouch of ash grew damp with his spiritually nervous sweat. He pulled his hand out and flicked the now ashy sludge away cagily.

Apex looked up at the soft rat-a-tat of the sludge as it hit the floor.
"Nandeo-desho-" Gozen groaned regretfully as all three of the Ulteriors pivoted towards the monks.

The personifications of Muiju Rikiku roughly carved into the Ulterior masks donned by Apogee, Apex and Apoc glowed due to their shining visages beneath them.

Apoc held up his hand to stop whatever machinations tried to begin within the cluster of monks.

Apogee placed her staff right above the crown of Thyaz's head, puncturing the circle of Khrystos that glinted fuschia upon contact with it. Apex and Apoc followed suit, slamming their staffs into the circle beside each of his ears. A faint golden triangle sprung up protectively on the floor around Thyaz's head that bloomed up into the pinnacle of a pyramid directly above his third eye in the space.

"Wait- they are honoring the-"
The Monks murmured among themselves that no move was made by the three interlopers to touch the actual body of Thyaz.

"They only want the-"

The Ulteriors looked up as a beam of golden light smashed through the ceiling of the dank space into the vibrational capstone of the pyramid. The dead eyes of Thyaz ripped open as his body convulsed in the fuschia circle of light as his soul slammed out of its shell.

Apoc motioned towards the Monks. Apogee, Apex and Apoc moved towards them as a unit.

The monks looked at one another and in a flash blew ash into each other's faces, disappearing in the dust. Rosaries and ladles full of holy water clanged noisily to the floor.

Khrystos came to shakily. His voice caught in his throat as he watched three things that technically couldn't exist outside of certain zones as they turned to face the still standing cluster of Comptrolling Missionaries who were too busy mourning the Rochet clad brother and the priest that Khrystos had decimated to notice the Comptrolling Monks had literally given up the ghost and left the building.

He sighed with relief when the pink glow of his protective circle registered to his strained eyes.

chapter fourteen

Someone nervously called up the corpse of Thyaz again high up in the D/o.

The fount of clouds that bloomed from the center of the D/o theater flickered chaotically between the harsh depravity of the reality of where his broken body was found and the spiritual battle that broke out over it in its aftermath. Everything was a headache inducing blur for the Denizens as it sped along.

"Wait! It's syncing back up!" The Tengu roared in the D/o theater as the feed jumped back onto its teeth.

"Wake up! Khrystos, come on , man!"
A hush fell over the crowd of Denizens as Khrystos groggily patched back into his spiritual brothers on autopilot due to coming to after having been totally off-lined.

"You can't be here! Your kind has no jurisdiction here whatsoever!" the cossacked priest roared into the masked faces of the Ulteriors on the feed. "That's why you hide yourselves! You know you have NO right to any of-"

An obviously female masked Ulterior slammed her fist into his bleating mouth.

The entire Demi-Ourgos Amphitheater momentarily winced. "Ooh!"

Everybody exploded into cheering, roaring with hearty approbation. "Who the fuck IS that?!"
"What the fuck is going on?"
 "Wait! We can cuss all the way now?! What in the -"

On the fount the other combative men of the cloth looked at each other, snarled and charged the woman, four on one.

"Now they're gonna jump her?! Oh Fuck that!Omg, I can Fucking cussssssss!" the Denizen Reyon howled happily. "Fuck! Fuck, Fuckkkk! This is crazy!"

"Wouldn't do that if I were-" a masked man drawled on the feed as the woman went berserk and ripped three of the four priests apart, "You." he sighed. The crowd went wild.

"That you'd even- You just saw her smash the throat of-" he shook his head as she angrily threw down her gloves and maniacally strangled the fourth priest with her bare hands wrapped in his own filthy rope girdle.

"You obviously went to Catholic school once, Apples~geeez" the other masked man muttered. "I mean, and I already know you're crazy but this is some deep-seated sh-"

"I was LeftHanded!"These fuckers and their fake gods! Fuck Them!" she roared crazily. More Comptrolling Missionaries flooded into the space and a spiritual brawl erupted between the toes of Khrystos and those of Thyaz.

Stupefied, Khrystos and all of those present at the D/o Theater via him watched as the Ulteriors made easy work of the brunt of the still standing missionaries. They ripped through them at lightning speed. A cluster of the Missionaries began to beg for mercy.

"Like the 'mercy' you sick fucks were going to visit upon his corpse?" the larger of the two Ulteriors hissed across the feed.

"Not the corpse, man!" Denizens yelled out in disgust.
"They were trying to Necrophilliac the fuck out with his- whathaveyous?!-"

"I'm sure it was much more specific a focus than random whathaveyousing-"
"Thank God we missed all that-I couldn't even-"
"I wanna see it-" a Denizen by the name of Qwan cheekily grinned in the dark.
"Shut up Qwan, No! Don't reverse the fucking feed, you sick-fuck is wrong with you?!" The Denizens around him erupted in laughter. "I tried to say Fucking feed but it's not forcing me to say fucking feed anymore- lemme- I flipped- Ok! Fuck! Fucking cool!"

"...Shhh!"

The main masked man looked up the shaft of golden light that steadily beamed into Thyaz's forehead and across the pizeoelectric sea at the center of his off-lined mind into his pineal gland, then up into the sky as if he'd heard the laughter.

"Fuck-"
A hush fell over the Denizens again as his eyes came back down and followed their sight line straight into the toes of catatonic Khrystos,

He whistled with a smirk. The other two Ulteriors looked up as he raised his finger solemnly to his mouth, then motioned towards Khrystos in case anything was recording them that could trace their voice patterns, Empyrean-wise.

The woman wordlessly killed another priest, making the leader override his own admonition.

"Apples, geez! WOMAN! We gotta leave some for the-" he did a bird call and motioned up. The Heralds on the roof stomped four times in unison to make their presence known.

The whisper of "And ...What the fuck is that?" rippled across the surface of the rapt Denizens.
"We'll find out soon enough, I'll bet-" was grunted from way up in the vertiginous nosebleeds.

"Fiiine! But let's fucking go! These fucking Pedales!" the woman snarled.

"You heard the lady-" the more sinewy Ulterior grinned.
"After you, my violent femme," the Diesel Ulterior demurred.
"Shut up-" she blush-grinned under her mask at their chivalry as she produced a thick brace covered in spikes with four sockets in it that glinted in the dimming light of the decrepit factory.

She opened it's latch and held it up perpendicular to the floor so that it looked like an odd halo and dropped it around the head of Thyaz. The golden light pouring into the pyramid stopped and changed directions, lifting the spirit of Thyaz up out of his fallen body by the face just enough for the halo to activate like a bear trap and slam into place around the neck of his soul.

A can of Heavenly tonic sloshed to the floor deep in the silence of the D/o theater.

Denizens shushed one another frantically and ducked behind seats as the woman paused and cocked her head towards Khrystos. "Hold up-" she murmured darkly and walked over towards the obviously AWOL Denizen.

"Come on, Apples! Don't Kill the-" the sinewy Ulterior began to fuss.

"Sonafabitch-" the other helmeted Ulterior yowled as the one they called Apples cold-cocked Khrystos.

The feed went momentarily black again, then completely dropped the signal.

Apogee smirked and sauntered back to the body of Thyaz, daring the Missionaries to make a move on her with every step. She bent down and retrieved her first casted staff and slid it into place.

Apoc and Apex followed suit and slammed the shafts of their staffs into two of the remaining three sockets. The outer spikes slid into the inner ring of the untouchable device around the neck of the soul of Thyaz and punctured its throat.

The wail that erupted shook the rafters of the old factory as he was coated with his own spiritual blood, cloaking him from Empyreanic detection.

"That should do it-" Apoc chuckled, "Let's go-"

The Ulteriors shot up into the sky with the soul of Thyaz strung up between him like a pig on spits.

chapter fifteen

"What does forever mean?"she asked.
"I dunno. I guess Us?" he shrugged.
"Oh!" She brightened up considerably. "I like Us!"
"Me too," he yawned, unfurling like the universe he was unto himself beside her. "I can't wait for Us-"

She snuggled all that she was outside of the structure of time against the universality that was him.

The singularity they'd spontaneously combusted into two from danced across the cooling surfaces of them like stars in the night skies of realms not fully formed.

"Me either," she yawned. Time came into being by her eyes watching the transit of her reply as it made its way to him.

She was transfixed. "Forever-" she whispered again.

"Forever," he echoed as all they ever were once evaporated into nothingness.

chapter sixteen

Dead eyes to dead eyes, it carried on. Weak ankles and knees popped to faint muzak and moans amid the sallow skinned crush of bodies awkwardly elbowing one another in both spotty and stark light. Bones creaked alongside the melodiously moist smacking of orifices suctioned to skin. Arms folded judgmentally across hairy, swollen, age spotted bellies that hung like stuffed shelves over flaccid penises peeking morosely out of heavenly male merkins as Citizens waited their turn.

Her eyes got jolted out of the redundancy of it all by the crackling of sparks across the bodies nearby. Her face was awkwardly wedged between a bloated appendage and the glass block floor that beamed all afoot in the four Ourgos chambers down onto the heads of the revelers who'd already taken their turns, if any cared to look up after having done their time.

The listless thwacking continued as she did her best to place the flashes sporadically scattering across all the bruised and naked bodies around her, like fixating on them in search of their meaning would drown out what had become hers after she'd won her campaign and been personally selected by Second Head as one of his own. The memory she was not supposed to have of his words rang in her perfect ears in time to the beat of flesh into a wall near her.

"A Beautiful One, seemingly engineered as such. Washed out to the point of being perfectly unobtrusive."

"Oh! It's the- there's a chandelier in here-" she whispered to herself, eyes rapt, drawn to the teardrops of crystal that shot prisms of light across the lewdly cavorting limp penises and arid vaginas that were of no use anymore where they were anyway.

All were slick with the oils they had streaked themselves in upon entering the four Ourgos chambers per perverse predisposition and predilection. Obscenely greased, the one heaving against her haunches slipped. He shoved her violently into the floor as if his ineptitude was her fault. She gritted her teeth and looked up through the tangle of condiment slathered limbs, still enthralled by the light bouncing off the chandelier onto the bodies. Put off by the rapturous look on her face even after he'd purposely rammed it down in an attempt to hurt her, the lecherous B.O that had once been a corrupt judge slapped her on the ass to release her from dutiful service. She slithered away before anyone could pull her back into the fray and charged the exit. Something made her stop shy of the doorjamb. She looked back at the crystals of the chandelier and the prisms that shot out from it across the upper reaches of the Ourgos pit and realized those had nothing to do with what she'd seen within the depths of the orgy she'd just washed up on the shore out of.

A weird twinge in her chest tried to stop her glance back down into the pit too late. The quicksilver webbing that her comrades seemingly were encased with just beneath the surface of their flesh pulsed in counterpoint to the prismatic effects caused by the chandelier above as they numbly plowed into one another. She looked blankly down at the scars across her forearm and began to float up out of the cottony, hypnotic fog in her head, in search of the fibrous glint she saw in the others under her own skin. A spark pulsated.

Startled, her left hand flew up to her mouth as her right arm wildly swung out to the door as she tried to brace herself. The downpour of saltwater all of the doorjambs of the Ourgos chambers had programmed into them washed over her ketchup, oil and excrement streaked body as she stood there in a daze. From that doorway she absently took in the entrances to the three other Ourgos dungeons.

Beautiful Ones who'd entered the Empyrean highs with H.O.E. tendencies towards necrophagy clustered around the lip of the Ourgos chamber outfitted with all things attendant to their proclivities, proudly brandishing gangrene streaks along limbs that were usually hidden among their brethren. The more sadistically wired on earth masochists and rapists licked their lips as freshly bound provisions were marched into the Ourgos of choice to whet the appetites of those who cued up for their allotted entries. The Ourgos affectionately nicknamed the UN was a cornucopia of racist fetishistic activity. Skull measuring, deviantly othering, sexual pathologizers compared crib notes as they waited in the wings. Scatophiles and urolagniacs roughly elbowed past her in the cascading doorjamb she hadn't moved away from.

She numbly made her way to the perpetually fogged reflective surfaces of the staging area and re-applied the mercury paste day of the dead skull makeup she'd arrived to the soiree in across her salty skin to replace all that had smeared in the Ourgos chamber, then anointed herself with l'eau du merde des Sauvages as the performative histrionics of her tribe effectively reduced themselves to the brown noise of the inescapable pathologies specialized in on earth vice gripping 2nd Head's Citizenry as unspeakably hollow necessities within the Highest High. The salt dried on her body before she slipped the simple, raw silk slip dress she'd worn under her reaper cloak to the party, the feel of the fabric not registering against her perpetually numb flesh. Still pondering the prisms of the chandelier and the webbing, she headed down the staircase into the crush of revelers, past the runoff from all four Ourgos zones that pooled at the top of the stairs and into a waterfall that emptied into the fountain on the main floor that the Beautiful ones greedily filled their ornately carved crystal cups from as the festivities raged on.

As she hit the main level her distracted, disinterested gaze catapulted her to the front of lines she had no comprehension of being in, the writhing bodies seen through the glass floors above her a crown of thorns from the perspective of the other almost seemingly beachy, salt-streaked Citizens who clocked her every move and all her eyes absently alighted upon in search of insight into the mysteriousness she'd finished doing her time glowing with. There was something there, something different about her, something that made the B.O's borderline obsessively latch onto in search of a strange proof of life that they'd have been hard-pressed to verbalize.

chapter seventeen

The shrieking began as soon as the lights flickered on in the decimated zone, indicating a night that came with no color change to the sky.

Very Important Pariahs wailed as they smashed each other into the fences around the courts, violently vying for the scantest whiffs of life they'd convinced themselves would somehow still be found in the eternally overflowing garbage bins lining the promenade along the caldera of fire.

In a twisted bout of King of the Hill their emaciated bodies were knocked off the writhing pile of Vipers pawing through the trash one after another like paper planes tossed towards the graffiti scarred ramparts of the dull glass tower. They slammed into its rickety foundations like the Deanimants they were.

They crumpled alongside the sluggish, fake Disavowed ones, Penitents who clawed at the decaying flesh of their VIP brethren between bouts of swinging their already partially crushed skulls at the tagged base of the building, howling in pain they didn't actually feel in hopes of triggering the raising of crosses they had once refused to bear.

The designation of the tower was split in two: Second Head of Council's Citizens occupied the front of the house while those disparaged as the Denizens of Third Head were relegated to the back of the house and below. Behind the tower, a brimstone cobbled alleyway spun from the shore of the caldera. Crumbling facades that would never gentrify in any sense of the word stood out like broken teeth across from the mausoleum-like, polished loft homes of the Citizens that gleamed with florescent light, spiritual prosperity cake-walking down a road that spiritual poverty had set up shop on long before it.

The silence behind the tower was in stark contrast to the fiery chumwalk churning on the side that the Citizens prized along the lake of fire. They'd slid along the caldera's boardwalk like ancient Druids in Reaper cloaks, many raw, ready and smeared with mercury based body paint that would not make it through the Quatro Ourgos if they had any say in how the festivities proceeded. The craven state of the Deanimant horde that lurched along the caldera reinforced post-Life pompous senses of superiority that the caste-like Citizenry within 2nd Head's camp of Beautiful Ones drunkenly brandished around the Empyrean, utterly soaked through to the bone with equal opportunity, self-satisfied contempt for anything not lucky enough to be them.

The most recently crowned the IT of Its, B.O./Empyrean-wise sailed through the writhing bodies on the promenade ambivalently, as invisible to the thrashing beasts around her due to her Reaper cloak as they were to her due to her outlook on life lived after life.

"And of course, she lives right on the edge of the Denizen zone," she muttered to herself as she apathetically stepped over a groaning Disavowed splayed on the ground, scaled eyes locked on the tower. Due to the Reaper cloaks the only thing the Disavowed saw when they looked in her direction was a reflection of the sordid afterlife they were strung up in, so most looked away.

"Anything for points," she sighed mockingly. "Oh, the courage! You must be so brave!"

She plowed hungrily towards the fawning of the sycophantic B.O's she called her friends, as addicted to feeding off the false piety and empty praise they plastered each other with in close company as the ones who had pedestaled her for being the current Queen of It were.

Faint whiffs of recognition dazed pockets of Disavowed ones as she passed until she came up behind the Penitents on their knees facing the tower's ramparts. The iron ore the Beautiful Ones anointed themselves with to block the scent of the quicksilver they doused themselves incessantly in per post Puryf protocol hung on her like an afterthought, like the smell of blood on a butcher.

The Penitents were still coherent enough to smell her for what she technically was, what she technically, possibly...likely... still had. Gape-mouthed, they froze. They were too terrified to be wrong and too hungry to chase away the hope of being right by gazing up at her as she sung out to alert her mates of her arrival.

The wails outside kicked up to a fever pitch to the joy of the Beautiful Ones above and the consternation of the Denizens in the bunkers beneath and behind the tower. The Penitent closest to the gate licked his fever blistered lips as she pressed her hand into the latch. He absorbed the vision of the sliver of mercury - laced wrist that peeked out then gagged, dropping into a choking fit on the stained concrete as her friends danced down and whisked her away in a cloud of indifferent laughter. He deftly wedged his naked, rot-mottled foot into the path of the gate undetected as the soiree door slammed shut, then slipped into the shadows of the Tower's outer vestibule and quietly pulled the gate closed behind him.

Inside the front facing tower the Beautiful One's bacchanal boomed. Heroically altruistic deeds were tossed into conversations like molotov cocktails flicked absently onto fires full of books burnt on bored nights. Fickleness fanned the flames of jealousy only they thought were hidden from view. The partygoers reeked of the decaying flesh and dirty sex they were all festooned proudly with as Libertines within the B.O camp.

The condo was filled to the gills with fetish objets d'art and primitive, appropriated masterpieces. She skimmed the cue up the back stairs to the orgies as she sauntered through the party towards the room that all reaper cloaks had to be piled in. Farthest from the door, they were put out of sight and mind like the gauntlet they'd all arrogantly pressed through to be there solely protected by them. Nouveau riche affectations dovetailed with fetishizing the Pentitently poor and downtroddenly Disavowed they'd all but mingled with in order to be there. They were aroused walking through them the way privileged on earth got whenever they'd ambled through areas decimated by drug wars to go party.

She wedged her way up the stairs through the blase press of fellow B.O.'s to the second level. Kama sutra and ancient Iranian sex manual miniatures blown up to movie poster size interspersed with Damian Hirst slaughter house photographs hung on the walls. Piles of discarded Venetian masks and multicolored merkins peppered the floor of the upper hall that spectator salons with bowls of keys outside of them spun off of as the hall marched towards the Ourgos chambers up front. Hollow, performative masochism comically echoed around her head thanks to speakers scattered throughout the party for those who waited their turned to dutifully do their time in the ditches.

The absence of bodily fluids factored into the food-positive camp of the Ourgos sex dungeons. Not one touch, smell or taste had broken through the purified sensory systems of all the B.O. Present. They were as technically untouchable as all else in the Empyrean since arrival, no matter how wildly they acted out against it on autopilot. Perversions even Puryf itself couldn't erase were allowed to run rampant sans consequence as part of 2nd Head's unspoken on recreational allowances for them.

She peeked in on the B.O. bondage boys as they jostled like warring elephant seals against the bruised male and female offerings that flapped around like fish out of water under them for their approval and felt a surge of pride over being their de facto ruler.

The poverty porn preening exploded as their current queen dramatically descended the staircase, the exquisite costume she'd painstakingly pieced together appreciated by those as fluent in the ancient art of cultural appropriation as she was. She hungrily inhaled the influx of energy the performative peacocking garnered. Unintentionally, a scattering of bored eye rolls and muttered protestations among those that otherwise lived for every ounce of pre-Emp historicity she flagrantly gave to the Gods registered too. Completely disoriented by it, she excused herself from her mostly doting fans. The taste of the waning of It's reign was always worst at first impact. It sunk into a pedestal-hogging prima donna's spirit with razor sharp teeth. An almost frantic upswing in posturing to recapture momentum among those who had only tolerated their dominion instead of those who had championed it sunk the star all the faster when witnessed by their raving fans.

Panicked, she swanned through the clutches of attendees helter-skelter, in desperate need of any flattery she could eke out of the awkwardly closing whirlpools of attention now borderline disgusted by the thirst for their attention her vibration now rung out with. She began to throw her head back a bit too uproariously to brayingly laugh at the cues the pompous Beautiful Ones peppered their tone deaf take downs of each other with. They decimated anything that did not line up with whatever causes were currently en vogue.

As the night went on, after being ceremoniously ejected with withering glances from every clutch of Ki-ki-ing terrible Citizens in attendance, she looked on in horror as all attention turned pointedly away from her. The Beautiful Ones had begun the coronation of the surely next to be christened "It" right in her face, as doused in disinterested distraction as she was drenched in the simplest raw silk that could hold whatever tale those that looked at her wanted to tell about her.

She looked down at the costume she'd so painstakingly pieced together solely for the pre-imagined joy of educating those who took her in on each aspect of it and felt slapped in the face. Her eyes ran back and forth between the dissolution of her abruptly castrated reign and the detritus roasting Disavowed ones outside, back-dropped by the churning sea of fire beyond the courts below. Her wrist began to itch with anxiety.

On the far side of the locked door Gangrene pressed his cauliflower ear against it and whispered chaotically.
She cried out as genius hit.

"Oh! Don't they look so hungry?!"she yelped melodramatically as she flung the glass doors that sealed the party off from the balcony open to the elements, wholly uncloaked. All activity on the first floor of the party as well as outside came to a standstill, except for her.

"What the-- What are you doing?"a Citizen near her whispered nervously.
"They- they just look so...hungry!" she cried out, moved by the surge of attention on her again, not the wretchedness of the

Disavowed that reminded the Beautiful Ones of their elevated station within the Empyrean.

"Are...are you hungry? You look like you're starving-" she sang down to them. She authoritatively called over her shoulder into the crush of the still stunned party-goers. "For 2nd Head's sake, someone give me some food to give them! And...could you, could you warm it up for them? That's right-"

The mounds of the Disavowed pariahs on the trash bins slowly stepped back from the lips of them and crept forward as the Penitents softly howled with joy. Their brother Gangrene inched down the outer steps and quietly opened the gate of the outer vestibule. The Penitents rushed in, rustling like dead leaves before slamming the gate behind them, drawing the attention of the last of the VIP piles who growled like beasts.

"See?! See how hungry they are!" the last It girl admonished the court whose new christening she'd successfully interrupted. "We can say we care to one another about the depravities of witnessed things, but until we lower ourselves to be the givers of the light within us that the Penitently and Disavowed truly need...we are just-" she sighed theatrically, "actors with bit parts half played-"

"What does that even mean?" a partygoer asked herself aloud as she shook her head. The Beauty scrunched up her face in confusion as she obeyed the gut nudge to casually and quietly back away from the front of the condo.

"Thank you!" It sang as the food the B.O's didn't even bother to warm for themselves since they couldn't taste it was passed to her.

A few more among the Beautiful Ones wise enough to override the vanity of being there inched down the hall after the confused Beauty to the back room where the heap of reaper cloaks were stowed and quietly shut the door.

The brunt of the poverty porn obsessed party goers on the main floor leaned in. They pressed towards the balcony to the point of having to push the glass pocketing doors completely open to accommodate their morbidly bourgeoisie curiosity.

chapter eighteen

The silence that descended was the only cue needed for the Denizens behind and below. "Here we go again-" Sid muttered.

She pushed heavy pieces of furniture up against the back walls of her bunker in case the shit that came with neighboring 2nd Head's "con-verts" hit as it tended to.

"Fucking ugly-ass heartless Beautiful Ones," she spat as she banged with her forearm on the doorjambs of every Denizen cell in her bunker. They mimicked the code for "Stay Inside" against the pipes that flowed down through the barracks built beneath the promenade to their neighbors.

"Again?!"
"Of course-"
"Could set a clock to this MESS-if time existed in this fricking hale hole!!"
"I'll case the back and set it-" Erythios muttered as he geared up. Maeve and Rotter followed suit along the perimeter as Sid looked around.

Sid flipped the warning brown breaker keyed to the tower and slowly counted off to herself.

chapter nineteen

The lights along the entire promenade and bunkers below it dimmed, then flared.

The few wise Beautiful Ones who scampered down out of back windows in Reaper cloaks saw it and ran like animals up the alley into their own territory.

The former queen of the Night, It-girl extraordinaire extended her warm food laden arms towards the Disavowed like an Angel of Mercy, performatively presenting the squinting hungry with the only thing they actually consumed as it held up her bounty.

It was the purest, most blessed offering of sustenance the Pentinents and Disavowed had ever witnessed in the Empyrean. The street lights along the promenade went out alongside all power to the tower.

The quicksilver lattices that caged the forcibly un-corrupted flesh of the Beautiful Ones glinted in the spiritual darkness for all the Disavowed to see in the absence of florescent light and reaper cloaks. They shifted as the Cornucopia of what they actually consumed revealed itself for what it was running along just under the surface of the former queen's skin.

They screeched and swarmed the open balcony of the abode of the Beautiful Ones like starved rats.

A frantic B.O. flung herself at the condo door and unlocked it, trying to escape the crush that poured in from the outside. She screamed as Gangrene and the Penitents pounced on her, dragging her down into the stairwell against the gate as those behind them climbed over their feast and poured into the soiree.

Throngs flailed on the far side of the gate as the Penitents feasted in every nook and cranny of the condo on whatever they could capture.

They shook the foundations of the tower as they climbed up and over balconies and bashed in windows with the already broken bodies of one another, the hunger overriding all else.

They kept what they killed and hunkered down in corners literally ripped the stuffing out of half conscious B.O.'s like the heavenly strawmen and woemn they were, pawwing through their bodies in search of the tangles of silky white filaments that returned to the Deanimants some semblance of grace.

They turned the upper reaches of the tower into a vomitorium of voracious consumption and defecation as they streamed through upper hallways sucking on the sanctified finger bones of those in one of 2nd Head's most favored clusters, in search of more of their preferred sauce.

chapter twenty

"Nice of you to join us-"

Thyaz and Artyo remained crouched close to the ground. The air around them shook silently from vibrations of laughter too high pitched to register to their ears. Their kamikaze jump covered approximately two feet and had been the entertainment for a grand meal that was taking place on the other side of it.

The entire space seemed activated by their presence, stuffed to capacity with supernatural beings folded down on what looked like the insides of ripped cushions. The mouths of the beings gaped open, the air in front of them resembling waves off asphalt in a hundred degree heat. Their bodies twisted in slow motion, each one seeming to freeze-frame itself in response to the eyes of Artyo or Thyaz on them.

As Thyaz's eyes calibrated to the atmosphere, Artyo's eyes strategically played over beings who moved with jagged grace, like they were slightly inebriated. She wondered if they walked like the newborn deer they moved like sitting down laughing at her. Bones in their faces seemed chiseled from granite. Almond-shaped Bambi eyes heavily fringed with lashes were painted blue, green and copper, and danced across their cheeks like peacocks when they blinked and eyed her curiously between silent guffaws.

Hair spun out from heads in woolly tufts or fell in silken sheets. Fleshy mouths revealed row after row of perfect teeth, some blackened, some optic white. Birds, dragons and snakes were etched in ochre across foreheads that gleamed as if they housed the sun. Tiny balls of liquid color raced after faces that had left them suspended in the air due to the sudden explosion of life in the room, as if the beings moved so fast that they took their make-up by surprise. Veins in hands glowed as they waved away the initial image of the two entering the zone. Eyes shot sparks as eyebrows aggressively slashed away from them. Bare skins in every shade seemed metallic, patches painstakingly painted with tar or quicksilver unreadable glyphs, others splattered with what looked like old blood. Artyo's retinas ached as they raced over folds of what had to be fabric woven from fronds of palm trees. Torsos were covered in what looked like puffs of cotton pressed between spider webs. Porcupine quills stabbed through leather that wrapped around legs and arms, and occasionally pierced them. Glinty coils of copper spun continually counterclockwise on fingers. Jewelry shape-shifted loosely around them with the life-force of whoever died to create such magnificent pieces. Fingertips and toes were dipped in latex, palms and the soles of their feet stenciled with cryptograms.

Thyaz clocked the space that surrounded them like the hustler he was. The surfaces of everything begged to be caressed, just like the exterior walls and the coppery sand outside had. The chamber was twice as wide as it was tall, and what looked like a glistening silk web draped from sandalwood rafters, creating the closet thing the room had to a ceiling. Thin vines snaked down from the beams to the floor, rotating slowly, creating an almost imperceptible vertigo once noticed.

The walls were sandstone, showing no mortar whatsoever. Meters up the walls were coated with black resin maps of the heavens cut into with flying discs in various stages of being swallowed by feathered serpents. The farthest wall opened onto an ornately carved trellis made of the same wood as the beams above, barely seen through hoards of nesting butterflies overlooking dense, low floating clouds that slid by. Cocoon-encrusted bridges danced along the horizon line on the other side of the caldera the space looked out onto. To their right, chunks of the hematite cobbled floor had been torn away to expose what looked like a canal that dumped into a pool then snaked towards the precipice the beings were casually camped out on. The banks of the canal were coated with more butterflies and piles of chrome disks that looked like hubcaps. Toy boats and lotus blooms bobbed in it. Beyond the canal burned a huge bonfire. The room smelled of teak, bamboo and charcoal. Small discs strategically suspended around the flames reflected light throughout. Piles of freshly cut flowers were scattered in front of the fire. Painted tigers paced around the flames sniffing at offerings, blood-stained fangs jutting out of the tufts of white hair around their mouths.

To the left, white fibrous clouds cushioned the beings who folded themselves around the side of the room that contained row after row of ebony planks levitating half a meter above the floor, draped in panels of royal blue silk.

Copper canisters full of twig chopsticks partially dipped in chrome dotted the tables. Cornucopias with every kind of fruit spilled onto tables. Baskets woven from green palm fronds overflowed with freshly burnt breads, charred roots, and black rice wrapped in leaves. All sorts of fish and small game roasted atop grates set into the floor. The black liquid of the canal gleamed like stars in blackened skies inside footless chalices balanced in tiny copper stands.

Another roar of silent laughter ensued as Artyo and Thyaz straightened up. Eyeing them as those feasting around her enjoyed a rare laugh not made at one of their own party's expense, the thrower of the feast was sprawled like a gigantic cat in the middle of the decadence. As the two regained their composure in what the host guessed must have felt like oppressive silence to them, her eyes followed theirs as they took in their surroundings, staking out the forbidden territory they'd entered into like tomb raiding thieves, oblivious to the one motionless Bodhi in the room. Her inky, black hair was held off her face by a blood-stained silk ribbon from the edges of her high forehead back for about half a meter. It twisted underneath the loose confines of the ribbon, seeming to go on forever beyond it, cascading down her into swirls on the floor. In the center of her glowing forehead was etched a spider in blood.

She watched them like the predator she was, the only brow she had arched mischievously over her left eye, a monocle balanced in front of it like a sniper's site on a thin copper chain that crawled down her back. Flushed lips silently mouthed the names of colors.

"Red-" Drops of red lacquer on her mouth atomized off her lips. The streaks of color and cryptograms pushed into the skin of her cohorts changed on her quiet command, slowly pulsating from blue, green, silver, black, white, then back to Ferrari red.

She sat enthralled by the possibility of an old trick gaining new fans like a child, wondering which one would be the first to realize that the colors of the costumes weren't changing being to being, but moment to moment. She made a mental note that the girl was the only one who seemed interested in the surface of the beings at all, and was not currently beguiled enough by any of them to allow her eyes to linger long enough to notice the effect. Her lips pursed as she silently flicked her tongue inside her mouth, whispering the word *de-sector* to herself.

chapter twenty one

"Laughter looks so fucking stupid when you can't hear it!" Thyaz telepathically snarked to Artyo. La Maestra could hear as if he'd spoken directly into her ear. Those spread out in front of them continued to melodramatically guffaw.

The host sputtered softly, trying not to laugh at the inside joke, then erupted. Her peal of laughter caused the beings around her to stare gape-mouthed as the ribbon unwound itself from her hair. Obscenely long tresses danced out and up towards the ceiling, blocking out the sky.

Artyo and Thyaz dropped to their knees in shock, hands slammed over ears, eyes bulging, cowering from the sudden explosion of sound from the thrashing wild woman neither had picked up on before.

"Funny! FUNNY-! THAT-" The Wild woman roared and slashed an arm towards Thyaz so sharply that he jumped as if something had been thrown at his head. His fear registered in her face and she blushed, then instantly regained her composure. "That...was funny," she finished quietly, swallowing the last of her giggles as her hair floated down from the rafters, trailing over everything and everyone around her.

Artyo stared at her, not sure if she wanted to laugh or cry.

chapter twenty two

Khrystos came to, trembling. He winced, then looked up in alarm as something on the roof shifted so methodically that his stomach flipped inside of his compromised spiritual shell.

The only Missionaries that remained had crossed the first Missionary murdering Khrystos off as eliminated. They paced around the empty shell of Thyaz, their broken brethren scattered haplessly around them, and took no notice of the plodding steps across the roof towards the skylight above them. The jabs at one another in their heated argument over who was going to have to explain what fell flat on the ashen man's body.

They dropped down into the space as a unit of four, facing out into the darkness, ANC boots cracking the filthy floor beneath them. The blood in Khrystos went cold as he tried to look away but couldn't.

The Missionaries hissed "What now?!" as they turned around towards the latest intrusion. Their mouths became thick with the final syllable as it registered to them what they were in the presence of. They quickly shielded their faces in horror.

Heralds.
Harbingers of the fiery abode of the Gods, the Empyrean enfleshed as far as any strung up between their Hell and that Heaven were concerned.

They were the closest petty HellonEarth Comptrollers like the Missionaries got to the concept of fearing the manifestation of the wrath of the violent Gods they trafficked souls on the supposed behalf of, known to be hell-bent on meting out their self-sufficient declarations of vengeance against middlemen of the cloth like them whenever they felt like it. Any comptroller that tried to escape them was always struck down for crossing unspoken on lines with unfinished business on the floor.

"Tsk, tsk~" The Head Herald muttered. "Even giving your kind time...to get your Comptrolling in order always seem to-"

"Amybalis, your Honor- I- I can explain-" a Missionary bleated.

"You DARE interrupt the High Herald, you Necrophagic Knave?!" The Harbinger roared two inches away from his nose. A sheen of sweat immediately broke out across the bridge of it as he threw himself on the ground and pleaded for mercy. "Forgive me, Our Father in-"

"Enough!" the Herald christened Meroe snapped. " Where is the special cargo your unit was assigned to-"

"Where is the sacred seed?!"
The remaining Missionaries fretted and softly stammered as they tried to explain. "What is this mewing?"

A craven priest began to sob and pointed wretchedly at Thyaz in the center of the room. Meroe narrowed her eyes and peered at the heap of empty flesh at the center of the space. She scanned him silently from his filthy broken feet to the oily hair on his head in search of anything that could corroborate that the one they hunted had fallen this far away from who and what he actually was. She breathed a harsh sigh of relief. Not him. She caught the eyes of the two tiered Heralds that reported to Amybalis alongside her, quickly shook her head no, then gruffly regained her composure. "This ...useless- Where is his Ba?" The Harbinger grunted.

"Or his Ka?" the one that was almost the spitting image of it growled. "What did you sick fucks Do to-"

"But-But-" the Missionaries fell into thundering protests and lamentations.

"Noba, no Ka… Only lecherous chasubles covered in splattered excrement and-" Amybalis wrinkled her nose "Blood? Spiritual Blood of your Own brethren?! Faction Infighting?!"

"No!"
"What, did they get in the way of your twisted delighting of yourselves in-"
"That's not what-" The Missionaries protested.
"Again?! You have the Audacity to interrupt the Head Herald with your bleating?!"
"I-I did noooo such thing!" A Priest argued back.
"Enough, Necrophage-"
"But we didn't-" they pleaded to be heard to no avail.

"Where is this Being's BA?!" Amybalis screeched like a banshee. "Or even the Ka?!" she roared as all the men of the cloth cowered on the floor behind the body of the Rochet robed fallen brother. "Where's the CARGO! Where is the cargo?!" she shrieked. Every human aspect of her countenance disappeared as she morphed into the terrifyingly wrath of God she'd strangled many a supposed prophet as for wasting her time.

"No seed?! No NEED for you consumptive carnivores!"

"Cannibals!" the Heralds raged as the cell violently smote the Comptrollers out of existence as per Empyrean retrieval protoco policy

chapter twenty three

"Get up," she commanded lazily in their direction.

She reminded Thyaz of the Pharaoh in the Ten Commandments as they scrambled to their feet. It was the first time he'd seen another woman fashioned along the lines of Artyo, and he was openly in awe. Artyo peeked out from behind him.

"You-" she inquired gruffly like a boy, pointing through Thyaz at Artyo and both of them knowing it, "Know where you are?"

"...Kinda-"Artyo whispered.
"...Have some idea, right...?" The wild woman with the spider on her head continued. Artyo nodded. The insanely long strands of black hair began to levitate and fold atop the woman's head of its own accord. The beings that had been frozen slid back into motion, eyeing Thyaz and Artyo as they ate their food in silence, curious.

"You are on the outskirts of the Empyrean-this," the wild one lazily gestured to the space around her, "is My territory within the Per-A complex. The house of Gold. My house..."

"Why are we in your house-?"Artyo interrupted. The woman furrowed her one brow as the monocle floated down and nestled into the binding under her breasts. Thyaz looked back at her as if she had lost her mind, his glare stopped by the strange look dancing in Artyo's eyes.

"You came through the equivalent of my sewers. Like thieves. Are you thieves?"the wild woman asked. Thyaz paused, wondering if things done in the past counted here. Arto shoved him to reply. He whirled around to glare at her. She telepathically whispered to him *"Answer her or die, again."*

The wild woman rolled her eyes. "I mean now- are you here to steal from me now?" she challenged them, brow raised.

"No!" they both exclaimed.

A snicker slipped out in the far corner of the room. "Are you here for assignment?" a lisping voice called out.
"Assignment for-?" Thyaz countered.
"Apparently not." the effeminate voice giggled.
Thyaz raised his own brows at the fact that he could now hear the laughter at his expense.

"You just taught them," the wild woman chuckled absently in reply to Artyo's confused look, motioning towards Thyaz, who blushed at expanding his audience. The bustle of food being wolfed down created filler between the pauses in conversation.

"What is your name?" Artyo asked softly.

The entire space stopped again. All turned towards the wild one. She rolled her eyes. "I am the weaver of worlds, etcetera, etcetera."

"That's not a- what is your name?" Artyo began again. The woman raised a finger to quiet her. Artyo drew back, shushed.

"Enough. Later. In my quarters. Sit! Eat!" she commanded. The beautiful,battle- scarred woman with the spider on her forehead turned her attention back to her food, which had grown cold. She looked up at the two causes of this, storm clouds gathering between the legs of the spider as her posse made space for them at her banquet.

"How do we know we can eat what they eat?" Thyaz mused to Artyo, sitting down cross-legged at the low table farthest away from the spider woman.

 Artyo yanked him down as the plate containing the wild woman's cold meal slashed through the air close enough to nick his right ear and draw blood before clattering to the ground near the bonfire, its contents pounced on by the feral tigers.

"BECAUSE-" the host roared from the center of the room. "Consumption is a atmospheric qualifier-" All the other beings paid close attention to their food, afraid to look up for fear of being smote on the spot. "If you were unable to consume YOU COULDN'T BE here. Even if you were here as an... offering." she laughed as her eyes danced over to her tigers. "You've come this far! Enjoy the ambrosia of the gods. Eat, eat, eat-!" she said softly, smiling the sweet smile of an angel as her fresh, hot food arrived.

Thyaz looked up at Artyo from her thigh, about to curse the woman. Artyo affectionately licked at the tiny trickle of blood on his ear and made a face. He blushed at her as she grinned, whispering eat, eat, eat to him in Spanish, Japanese and pig-Latin all at once, clogging up the sector they were being spied on through. He sat back up timidly, shooting the wild woman a baleful look before a scent akin to Korean barbeque hit him. Realization of the famine they'd moved through set in. The two of them descended on the fruits closest to them like animals. Nectar from a huge peach dripped off Artyo's chin as she watched Thyaz scan grills containing meat.

A being across the table from them sneered, raising his chopsticks as if to roughly jab Thyaz. "Over there-" the being motioned listlessly to the left. The bodhi snorted then rolled his eyes at Artyo's warning glare. "You don't go after it! you- call it to you-" he sighed, exasperated. "You decide what you want to eat," the bodhi continued abrasively, his demeanor softening when he felt warmed by both pairs of eyes on him, "and it comes to you," the being continued gently. "Like this."

Chunks of charred flesh were suddenly sitting right in front of them both. Thyaz nodded at the being and tore into the food, causing Artyo to chuckle as she looked on. The being blushed when he realized that she was still looking at him.

"Do you wish to call something from me?" the bodhi whispered softly. He lowered the lids of his eyes, causing the fringes around them to throw spiny shadows across his cheeks. Thyaz glared at her over his food, daring her to even think about flirting back with whatever it was.

Artyo grinned back at the being. "What are you...?" she asked softly.

Thyaz narrowed his eyes, thanking both of them that she hadn't asked who, the way she'd first done with him, which would have made him have to kill all three of them. Artyo raised her eyebrows and thought *Simmah down!* Thyaz went back to his food. The blatantly male being leaned over the table towards her, intrigued.

"What is a Simmah?"

"He is- he's simmering." she blushgrinned and motioned to Thyaz. Placated, Thyaz kept feasting. "What are you?" she repeated.

"One of them..." he whispered, motioning over his shoulder at the beings behind them. As Artyo looked at the Others, she was suddenly taken aback by the fact that all of them were suddenly wearing white instead of the various colors their gear seemed to have been moments ago.

"Took you long enough-!" the wild woman chortled many tables away.

"Oh- and they are-?" Thyaz asked gruffly around a mouthful of food.

"Nefilim-" the being said quietly.
"Necro what?!" Thyaz snorted.
"Nefilim," the being murmured to her as he raised one of his spindle-like fingers up to dance across her chin and peered into her eyes.

Thyaz lunged across the table. Incensed, the being lunged right back towards him, gnashing razor-sharp rows of teeth as if he intended to rip Thyaz's flesh from his body.

"Flipth-" The host gurgled absently to herself over the first bite into what had to be the best mango she had ever eaten.

Instantly, both Thyaz and the bodhi were strung up in the air, frozen an inch away from each other's grip above the table, bodies forcibly twisted. Their grimaces of pain triggered snickers throughout the den. The wild woman set them down in each other's seats in states of embarrassed shock.

"What is a Nefilim?" Artyo asked again as if nothing had occurred. Thyaz glared at her. The Bodhi looked into Artyo with the calmest eyes she had ever seen.

"Well, you were-once." the Bodhi whispered sagely, turned away and tried to concentrate on drawing his food.

chapter twenty four

The Spiderwoman's feast continued without incident until she excused herself and headed towards her chambers.

"As is the custom," the bodhi now seated next to Artyo whispered upon noticing her eyes following her departure.

Wild-eyed and full, the barefoot woman dragged her mantle of chromed porcupine skins on the polished stones behind her to a black gash that Artyo hadn't noticed before in the wall to the far left. She mind-gripped two of her more esoterically endowed consorts as she made her way. A pained moment of silence settled across the space. Heads peered down into laps and then looked up to the red sky that became more visible with every step the Spider woman took away from the festivities. Artyo and Thyaz looked around at the statuesque beings ensconced in what had to be prayers. They looked like a flurry of snowflakes frozen in a high speed snapshot, back-lit with searing red light. Then suddenly, the Spider woman was gone.

The Nefilim wondered who would first break into the revelry that went with the hunting party returning home from the chase. The Nefilim who had Sensei'd Thyaz was the obvious choice by the winks and nods of his brethren.

He suddenly sprung up onto the balls of his left foot, knee bent, right leg extended out in front up him at an awkwardly beautiful angle. His hands flew to cover his face and then danced gracefully above his head. His eyes glazed over and his lips became caked with blood after he bit into himself, willing the balance to continue. With one fell swoop, Sensei slammed down into fetal position. The bacchanal broke out as soon as he hit the floor.

The beings began guzzling the black liquid at an alarming rate, some pulling out flasks that they submerged in the canal itself to fill before tucking them into the folds of their gear. Their hunting costumes became as shiny and black as the liquid they gorged themselves on, as if the tiniest strands had been dipped in liquid latex. Even the brandings, tattoos, and cryptogram graffiti scrawled over skins began to gleam black.

"What was this?" Artyo asked the cluster of beings that had made their way around her to preen like oil-slicked birds.

"A celebration of a realm we'd lost faith in ever seeing again-"
"But we returned with forty members of the party! Unprecedented-"
"Eons have passed since I have felt the texture of my own Per-AEmpyrean silks across my skin-"
"There was so much blood to release prior to re-entry-"
"You see the beauty in hindsight, and release the pain of the process-"

Thyaz marveled in silence at how the beings fought for audience with Artyo and how she sat in the midst of what he could only call visual insanity and looked so perfectly at home. He decided to focus on anything besides her obvious comfort among entities that were so beautiful that they hurt his eyes, entities who roamed around like wild animals when they know there is no need for them to be on guard. They were creatures with lines he had never known to exist outside of the reflection he'd hated in his own mirror his entire life in what he sat there starting to believe really was hell after all.

Ebony planks went flying into the pyre as Artyo and Thyaz continued to eat. Fish were lifted up by the tail, animated and tossed off the balcony into the unseen crater-lake below. The piles of white the beings had been sitting on were thrown out over the trellis, floating upward against the red sky. More pillows were ripped open and tossed out. Insides went up, silken blue cases liquefied and dropped towards the churning waters below. They enjoyed both the spectacle of the room being ripped apart and watching the pyre tigers wildly splashing into the black liquid to get to the chrome discs the remaining food was floated towards them on.

The beings began to whirl around the cleared space like wild, spiky spinning tops. They dervished, everything loosely draped upon them corkscrewing around them, hair, mantles, arms and legs, all chaotic pulsating motion. Sounds exploded through the tops of their heads. Notes reeled into one another, strains coagulating in pockets across the cobblestones into music, a hybrid of what they called up out of each other in joy at finally being home, whatever this home of theirs was.

Artyo sat in awe. The only time they stopped dancing was to guzzle directly from the canal like ravaged beasts, dunking their heads into the blackness haphazardly, drawing away from it with splatters of the liquid coursing over the tops of their skin before being absorbed. Those who'd been twirling alone began vibrating suggestively at those nearby. Pairs gyrated around one another ambisexually. Music throbbed through them as they whirled in front of Artyo and Thyaz, grinning lewdly. The swerve of it all pulled at the clubland energies in the two of them as they tried to stay put, enjoying the cacophony without physically losing themselves and one another in it. Artyo looped her fingers into Thyaz's as she felt the jarring rhythm take hold of her senses. The closer they danced to her, the more she spun out of control. Thyaz couldn't tear his eyes away from the spectacle. He watched as the ones that were most likely female aggressively ripped gear off the torsos of the ones who had to be male, never missing a beat. Myn snaked around womyn who straddled the floor and moved as if they were thrusting against giant invisible beasts. Circles that always sprung up around those going for broke in nightclubs were nonexistent. Attempts to make those feeling the most freedom from the music to become self-conscious by those able to only pose had no place here. They were all in on it, keyed into anything brazen enough to enter the dance with them.

Artyo turned from the near orgiastic scene with tears in her eyes, head filled to capacity with the combined wails- she had no other terminology for the sound that was emitting from them- that hung somewhere between hard-core industrial house and a violent waltz. She watched the fire in order to catch her breath, absently following the rivulets of copper and silver pooling around it due to the metals melting in its flames. She imagined the ores slowly trickling back into the mountain, different materials coursing counter clock- wise into it. Replenishment. She looked up as the Nefilim who'd taught her the lay of the land crawled out of the fetal position on the floor towards them.

"You are being requested in the interior chambers."

Thyaz stood up and stretched himself then pulled Artyo up. They walked towards the slash of palpable darkness ripped into the wall. A few paces ahead of her, the hair on Thyaz's neck began to stand on end in response to the sound of chanting pressing out at them. As Artyo reached him, head thrown back eyeing the blackened carvings on the wall instead of paying attention to where she stepped, she ran into the sinewy arm he stretched out to block her from falling.

 A bridge of ebony planks like the tables lay linked together by strips of copper spread out where the room dropped off. It had to be stepped down onto to access.

"Don't look back" she whispered to him softly, nudging him forward.

chapter twenty five

After they had left, the Nefilim that had interacted with Artyo and Thyaz stared out at the cocooned walkways suspended beyond the balcony as those around him frolicked eagerly with each other.

He found himself wishing for the first time in this existence, wishing that she'd asked him what precisely a Nefilim was because to answer that was the only way he'd ever be able to find out himself. Here. Thoughts, questions he'd never known he had ricocheted dangerously in him as his brethren christened him Sensei, calling out to him affectionately as they danced all over the place.

The moniker slapped him with the reality that the one time he'd been given direct audience to minister to someone legally sanctioned to ask him anything had slipped through his fingers. His sinewy arm shot up over his head in frustration. He slammed his fist down in protest. Howls of rage choked him. The ribbons that had selectively sheathed his obscenely long dreadlocks at their roots began to unravel. The snake chasing its tail tattooed onto his forehead glowed for a split second before evaporating off his skin, leaving pale scarring across it. Slowly, the glyphs on his skin began to shift. Some faded, other seeped into his flesh. The spider web-like tunic encasing his upper torso went ashy then dissolved into dust, followed by his pants. The stiff leather weight belt encircling his stomach fell open and off of him. His lungs expanded to full capacity for the first time in forever, above. He threw his head back and roared in pain in the middle of the festive room.

His brethren froze. They turned towards him, honoring the pained cry with the silence it commanded.

Sensei stood up solemnly, naked except for the copper bands twisted into his neck and the tattoo coiled around the belly button that he'd never known he had, another snake chasing its tail. He looked at the bonfire on the other side of the room. Pain felt for the first time morphed into tears of joy as he slowly walked towards the flames in the oppressive silence of his kindred.

"Sensei!" they began to chant rhythmically, encouraging him onward, upward. Down.

The fingers on his right hand twitched as if whatever careened inside him was hitting strings on a never before used instrument. The fingers of his left played gently over the mark of human divinity that had been on his stomach the entire time.

"I will lead with this one," Sensei whispered aloud to himself, pausing to look at his long right fingertips gleefully. He laughed as the interlopers had laughed.

The Nefilim around him exploded into thunderous cheers as he broke into a sprint towards the pyre. He saw he had already gained a tangible comprehension of space as he cut through the air. Dimensions below what he'd vibrated on as a Nefilim popped out in relief everywhere he looked.

He saw what he- they- his clan- must have looked like to Artyo and Thyaz and yelped happily as he lunged for the fire. The roar from his Nefilim brethren echoed in his ears as his bodhi exploded into blinding light upon hitting the flames. They were the last sounds he purely heard.

The beings covered their eyes with their hands, peeking shyly through fingers in awe at the fireworks. They had no clue what had caused it. But they understood that the one they wordlessly knew as Ourobouros was no more, freed from this level by the flames that licked higher life off the closest thing he'd had to flesh as one of them.

Dust to dust.

His ash mixed in with the metals pouring out of the base of the pyre. His sense of self moved among the molecules of copper and silver, atoms melding with them after so many millennia of separation. On the way down.

Slowly, in the back of the room, one who remembered yet wanted to forget began to spin again.

The festivities returned to their feverish pitch in the blink of an outrageously fringed eye.

chapter twenty six

A heavy darkness suctioned onto every inch of them, climbing up their noses, corkscrewing deep into ears, between fingers and toes. It blocked out all the sound they'd been swimming in a split second ago. Every muscle in Thyaz's body went into spasms before they slammed into the beginning stages of rigor-mortis. Artyo wrapped her legs and arms around his, lost somewhere between protective instincts and all-out terror.

Feeling the darkness aggressively push against the fabric barely covering her crotch, Artyo opened her mouth to scream and choked on the darkness that pressed forcibly against her throat. All that kept them alive in the belly of whatever beast they'd entered was feeling the strained pulse of each other. Artyo forced the two of them into a slow, painful crawl forward, dizzy from the absence of oxygen as she dragged the front part of Thyaz forward with her arms and pulled the remainder of him with her thighs and pelvis.

"Fuck it!" she screamed internally then swallowed.

chapter twenty seven

Meroe and the tiered Heralds shot up into the atmosphere empty-handed. Amybalis paused and called out over her shoulder towards where Khrystos lay broken and paralyzed with fear due to what he'd just witnessed.

"FUGITIVE-" she growled softly.

Any ability to speak that had been had by Khrystos disintegrated in time to having witnessed the Heralds smote each and every one of the Missionaries, even the already crossed ones, to ensure they'd not be re-conscripted. "Your discernment of the nature of the precipice upon which you found the precious cargo...stopped it from ceremoniously being irreparably defiled, Fugitive- by that holy scourge-" Amybalis seethed.

Khrystos twitched uncontrollably as his life and afterlife flashed before his eyes.

"Due to that discernment, you have gained your right of passage-" The head Herald whispered. Khrystos emitted a pained howl. "You know that ANY of you AWOLs we Heralds come across fireballing we're supposed to drag back to the Emp and fire in the hole the last bit of skittish light out of you so you'll stay put, but… Consider this your get out of Retrieval Free card. And... Stay out of dodge-"

Amybalis looked at the aftermath of the carnage and detritus the roughly de-scaled, flickering orbs of Khrystos had seen against his spiritual will and padded over to a bamboo ladle abandoned by the intervening Monks when they'd fled the Ulteriors. A smidgen of sacred water rested in its corner. Amybalis picked it up, went over and crouched in front of Khrystos sprawled in the muck with his spiritual cage cracked open, spiritual body wracked by the kinesthetic fits often triggered by scales on spiritual eyes falling inward instead of out.

"Breathe, child," Amybalis whispered. "Looks like you were borderlining before you saw naan a smote or Tding," she muttered almost tenderly as she gingerly caressed Khrystos's bruised cheek.

He burst into tears of blood that burnt away flesh as they slid down his face, revealing the tattoo of the Ensign rank he'd originally rallied under and deserted. She narrowed her eyes in soft shock. He'd been through enough.

"Consider this an...exculpation of sorts, a temporary Shrift, even." Amybalis whispered, "but stay out of dodge."she growled again. She tilted his chin up with one hand and solemnly drizzled the sacred water into the eyes of Khrystos to put him out of his misery. He let out a blood-curdling scream.

"Breathe Through it...Khrystos-" The High Herald whispered as the AWOL blacked out.

chapter twenty eight

In the distance, hazy cumin and thyme covered hills echoed the shapes and shadows they'd picked their way down through to enter the valley what felt like many lifetimes ago. To look back after having walked forever became too demoralizing because it never seemed they'd gotten very far. To look forward was overwhelming because the ridge ahead was so desired that it had to be treated like a known mirage to stop the heart from giving out. So they paid attention to their steps so intently that any semblance of pressure shift from night to day that used to set their spirits on edge no longer registered. Keyed into now, their trust beamed out of them and lit their path.

Until the estuary.

Espresso brown as harsh as winter whirled with a rich, autumnal ochre and stained green algae as bright as spring in the humid atmosphere, hung as heavy as if it were summer streaked across the area. The saturation of all surfaces made the permeability of the place soak into her as they picked their ways around the edge of it, the heaviness in the air only bearable due to the frenzied reminder of swarms of wild birds flapping wings as they circled above then flew away towards targets. Dander from the last cloud of birds their presence had made shoot up into the sky stuck to their exposed skin in shocking heat that should have evaporated all the moistness surrounding them, but somehow didn't.

She remembered the last paved road she'd seen in a flash. Due to choices she'd made, choices that had carried her through barely hospitable yet somehow vaguely safe lush terrain, she'd been above it. Alone, muttering to herself, looking down on the road she'd eschewed. It was stained and cracked, coated with the dusty last gasps of barren foothills that crumbled alongside it. Yellow streaks down its center were faded, eaten away by the atmosphere. But in that landscape along that road the goldenrod paint on the old asphalt soothed parched eyes like a shot of wildflowers. The more recently repaired places gleamed black where they weren't streaked with dirt, writhing like inky splatters on pristine paper in the waves of heat that rose up off the road.

Her eyes darted between yellow and black tar erratically, whispering to her like it was an eloquent, pregnant, visual language. Her mind raced with how used to being shunned on this journey she was due to how she walked it out, remembering how many names and insults she had absently deflected as she picked her way along the edge of the precipice she'd found her way to by herself. "From all those people," she muttered aloud, then froze. The silence registered. "Wait- what the hell?" she yelped. "That road … that road was packed! Where did all the-"

She looked back over her shoulder at the black stains on the road. "Oh my God- They're-" she squinted, "They're pits! they're fucking-"

A bruised, blood caked hand reached up out of the road, grabbing blindly in response to the sound of a voice on the wind. Any voice. Her voice.

Her hand slammed over her mouth as screaming under the road exploded. Her eyes adjusted as they raced up and down the stained road from above. The reality of what the larger stains were punched her in the stomach. "Blood- swarms- ripped to shreds by-oh my god-" Her horrified whisper caught in her throat as they'd come around the bend and made their way down the road. The screaming that had roared like the wind stopped.

Strangers. Obviously. Awkwardly alongside one another on the far side of whatever they had battled through to get there. She frantically picked up rocks and threw them down to get their attention, any fear of something possibly being above her trumped by what she now understood was below.

He saw her. Her panicked energy hit him so viscerally that his hair stood on end. She motioned them up. He reached out to the petulant guy he'd made it through hell with.

"What now?!" he snapped, completely over the comforts company had temporarily given them both. He'd pointed up to her and pantomimed climbing as the wind seemed to kick up around them. "Oh, now you can't talk? You've been going on the-" the exhausted man moaned as it dawned on him chatty Cathy was miming they needed to climb. "What the fuck do I look like, a Fucking Goat?!" he spat.

"We finally come to a fucking road and now you suddenly
Silently wanna climb?! How the fuck are we supposed to get up
there?!" his partner brayed, his pissed off voice booming.
His eyes had bugged out of his head as it registered that the
howling wind faded with the sound of it.

"Come on, man something's not-" he whispered hoarsely, face
ashen.

"You don't even know her, you horny fuck! After saying no to
what iii- you're such a fucking twat! You fucking 'Bro- Who
knows what kind of bitch that is?! All you see is she's alone!"

The screaming wind popped again like a chorus, howling in
agreement with his partner as it seemed to fill his petulant pause.
Spooked, he'd backed away from the road up the crumbling
incline as his partner pitched a fit.

"No! No!We've already climbed through hell! We're finally not
dusty and That's fucking only because it's so fuckin humid now
that the sweat has made it drip off of us!" he roared. "We finally
come to a fucking road- a real, paved fucking road, there's finally
some sort of breeze-" he railed as the winds kicked up again.
"And you want to go get all fucked up in the dirt again?! Fuck
no! No!"he roared up at his ex-partner as he clawed his way up
towards where she stood, frozen. "You can Have him, bitch! I'm
done climbing fucking dusty-assed mountains! I'm not going
anywhere beyond this fucking road! Fuck yall!" his former
partner snarled as he turned to march on the road he had chosen.

Hands shot up out of the shadowy kregs and grabbed each ankle
as soon as he put his foot back down.

"What the fuck?!" he screamed as both sets of hands roughly yanked him down onto his knees. More hands shot up, clawing the air in search of him, determined to pull him through the street even if he had to be torn in two to do it.

He'd fallen on his ass in horrified shock and frantically kicked his way up the hill before he'd turned and scrambled away from the assault below like whatever was left of his life depended on it, leaving his former road partner exploding in terror on the cracked asphalt.

"Help! Help me! Come back, you sonafabitch! You fucking cunt, why didn't you tell us?!" his ex-partner had screeched. "You fucking cunt! I'll see you in fucking hell!" he roared chaotically as he waved his arms wildly overheadd, slapping away filthy hands blackened with old blood.

She had stood on the precipice and watched the carnage below, rapt. The one left behind cursed and fought the grabbing hands off viciously. He panted between animal-like whinnying that seemed to energize whatever was pulling at him from below. More arms shot up on either side and dug nails into his torso. Hands grabbed the waist of his cut off jeans and violently yanked his upper body down onto the road. His face slammed into it awkwardly as he groaned in pain. Blood gushed into the road as he lifted his destroyed face up, disoriented.

The screaming stopped, stilled by the blood pouring down into the darkness. The hands on him loosened as everything below ran to where his life-force rained down. Stunned by breaking his nose he whipped his head around groggily before the jaundiced, beady eyes dancing around hungrily in his dripping blood below registered. He shrieked and jumped up, running towards the two of them above as his friend finally made his way up.

He had looked down in shocked confusion as his blood coated companion ran down the road, howling as he flailed in a panic. He'd retched.

"Get off the road! Off the road!" she's screamed from overhead. Those underground roared so loudly that the ribbon of asphalt undulated with the vibration of it as whatever they were set out after him like sharks trailing chum as he ran down the road.

"No! Off the road, you asshole!Get Up! Up! Come up here!" he'd yelled. His partner pivoted and broke into a run towards the foothills.

"Yes!Yes!" they'd screamed, waving him up as he got close to the edge of the asphalt.

His foot landed squarely on one of the shadowy splatters of previously murdered road trippers before him and he tripped. Multiple arms shot up out of the hole and yanked him violently into the ground as they'd looked on in horror. The roadkillers slammed his body into the rough edge of the hole again and again until he was unrecognizable as anything but pulp, then ferociously yanked what was left of him down into it with them.

His friend had passed out as she puked.
They'd been together ever since.

chapter twenty nine

The sacred water crested on the inner lids of Khrystos before all that was plummeted into a black, craggy abyss. The droplet gained momentum, glistening in the dark chasm until it slammed into the third eye of Khrystos and erupted, ripping it open.

The D/o theather watched the glistening orb as it sliced through the fount of clouds in reverse. They all froze as it hurtled towards them. "What is happening?!" a Denizen by the name of Dyn whispered harshly.

Everything went mute as the droplet barreled into the protective field strung up between it and its target.

Without warning, the fount exploded upon impact. Droplets from the spray of it landed on all eyes present as all the Denizens try to get out of dodge to no avail.

All power to the Demi-Ourgos Amphitheater went out. It was the first time since its inception that the Kahnic fount had ever been interrupted, let alone exploded.Ever.

"What is the Hell have you all done now?!" Sifu screamed from deep within the complex. "Wait- did I just say hell?!"

His hand flew over his mouth. "What in the-"

chapter thirty

Pressure receded as quickly as it had pushed against them, satiated by the offering of Ourobouros on the other side of the wall. The room exhaled.

Thyaz found her face and rammed his mouth against hers. The more she attempted to squirm away the more vice-like his panicked limbs gripped her. Artyo felt her muscles go rigid due to the aggressiveness as rage spiraled up her back. She blindly kicked away from him, the heel of her foot connecting with his solar plexus. He went flying. Artyo lunged and pinned his shoulders down with her knees as he laughed at her counterattack. Enraged, she slapped him, shocking both of them. "Dont DO that!"she screamed, "Don't EVER-"

The deranged laughter of the Spider woman rained down on them out of the darkness. " Is this how you two~ you know?" she chortled from above.

Slivers of red light began broke through the darkness and bounced off of the damp stone floor the two of them hadn't noticed. Thyaz shoved Artyo off of him and glared at her through the haze. Artyo opened her mouth to protest but slammed it shut as the space around them suddenly boomed with chanting.

"What the f-" Thyaz snarled as they ran back to one another.

 Above, gigantic crows cawed angrily at being disturbed. The remaining blackness around them dissolved into full-on red with the flutter of their huge blue-black wings, revealing the giant cage-like domed space Artyo and Thyaz had ended up in the bottom of. The open weave of the cage matched the Star of David motif on the pants of the wild woman who chuckled as she peered down into gigantic nests that lined the uppermost perimeter of cliff-like steps that climbed up towards the top of the open-air Geodesic dome.

She leapt from the ledge of nests onto a swing hung above the heads of Artyo and Thyaz, rocking back and forth as the crows re-situated themselves in large pockets along the rungs of a giant cage positioned over an ancient amphitheater. The wild woman whispered incantations down onto her captive audience as they looked up in horror at thirteen humanoid shapes wrapped in gigantic silk cocoons suspended overhead in front of the swing. Glistening limbs and tufts of hair protruded at bizarre angles from between the wispy threads. The heads of her two most recently chosen ones poked out from the bottoms of the ones closest to Thyaz. He recoiled in disgust before their ecstatic countenances drew him back in for closer inspection.

"It's not what you think-" The wild one purred. "I've no use for the things you're currently imagining." The murmured chanting boomed again.

Dropping away from where they stood were trenches filled with row upon row of softly wailing, feral holy men smeared with giant crow shit, foreheads aflame, blackened mouths hung open in agony. They were jaundiced no matter the skin colors and creeds represented among them. Artyo stared, as enraptured by their indecipherable howls as she was by their constant rocking and sticky nakedness.

"Getting it all out of them so they can do no more harm when loosed." the wild one answered without being asked. Artyo peered back up at what reminded her of what spiders spun around their eggs. "This... is about purification, preparation for the holiness of wars righteously waged," The wild one began. "For some it happens through one process, a birthing" she whispered and motioned to the those suspended. "For others, the path turns in on itself..." she chuckled, absently waving in the direction of the religionists rocking in pits dug into the ground by their own hands. "Some," the wild woman continued, gesturing overhead towards the crows, "get to fly right through it...while others...can...how is it said? Walk into the belly of it. It just depends-"

"What are you going to do to us?" Thyaz snapped rudely. The wild woman looked at him incredulously.

"Us? There is no use here for You whatsoever," she said dismissively, wounding his ego. "However… You-" she murmured, eyeing Artyo, " the Anannke needs for herself-" she purred gratuitously.

Thyaz's skin crawled. "What is the Anannke?" he snapped. The wild one raised her single brow at the two of them. "You Are in the Anannke's Per-A purification complex-" she began as if hypnotized.

Artyo broke in. "Wait-Nooo-We are here- with you-you- but You are not the Anannke! It doesn't make any sense for you to be the Anannke- you're too young-"

"Who the fuck is Anna Kaye?" Thyaz screamed at the top of his lungs. The whimpering of those in the floor stopped but both women completely ignored him.

The Spiderwoman's eyes clouded over. Her voice went soft with confusion that would have made her consorts on the other side of the wall implode."Then who am I?" The wild one whispered almost shyly.

"What?! You're doing all this PURIFICATION-" Thyaz raged, "All this...Whatever the hell this is- And you don't even know who you are?!- and Why are you asking her?! This is making no kind of sense!"

He looked over at Artyo, who stared up into the face of the wild one in shock. "Chola," he whispered to her, "What's going on? How could you know her name if she does not know it?" he asked.

"It can't-it can't be-that- was-wasn't- I don't-understand" Artyo whispered as memories spun erratically across her face. "Kagome Arachne...her name is Kagome-Arachne." Artyo whispered, mystified.

The gigantic crows exploded into abrasive caws as Kagome swooned on the swing. A bewildered smile of self-recognition spread across the Spiderwoman as she swung wildly on her perch above them and sung out insanely, a spell broken.

"As told to you by Kagome Arachne, Weaver of the web that holds all worlds in place, The Force behind Necessity, who dances within the meridians and in whom the meridians first danced!" she bellowed, newly re-christened. Kagome pulled herself into lotus position on her perch, mumbling her names to herself again and again as she took out a knife and carved each name roughly into her forearms so she'd never forget them again.

She abruptly stopped. "The Anannke summons you-" she growled softly as Artyo and Thyaz dissolved back into the blur of white- hot reality that had initially overtaken them upon slamming through the spinning swords.

chapter thirty one

Khrystos awoke in a daze in a vat of boiling water that did not burn him. His orbs flickered from black to white as his head bobbed passively in it. He raised his left arm to groggily wipe at his face, only to see his hands were drenched in skeins of wet silk in the churning water.

"What the-" he gasped. It turned into a gag and he retched out more and more skeins into the giant cauldron. He was adrift in it. He pulled frantically at the clumps, horrified as it spewed out of him, even as he rejected it- until it became his new normal, boomeranging back and forth between peaceful droughts of sweet air and violently purging into the pool he was in.

Only when emptied did his eyes start to take in his surroundings.

The wet, clammy black walls seemed porous, like lava stone that inhaled and exhaled in opposition to his own labored breathing pattern. Tree stumps glistened brown and green in the steam from whatever he sat waterlogged in. Wet, gaunt bodies were gingerly pulled up out of the vat by things he couldn't see and hung on a wall with a giant bamboo rack they were draped across to dry out in front of a bonfire. He shivered in fear as he watched his fate until he made peace with the pending path. Surrendered.

Emptied of his last silky skein Khrystos was pushed beneath the surface of the churning water again, all the way to the bottom of the vat. The riptide under it wrung whatever else was left in him out. He came to as all that was left of what he'd known himself to be in the afterlife sailed through the clammy atmosphere and he was draped, the same way he'd seen all other draped prior to him.

From his higher vantage point he saw black mulch, bare gray willows and laurel trees that started to shoot teeny green buds out almost as if in response to the press of his eyes. He latched on to them, then the shadows of tree branches that looked like skeletons.

The pyres of Yerba Santa that dried all things on the rack pulled him in and out of visions without warning but at least he felt no pain and had no memory. His eyes followed streams of smoke up into a sky he'd forgotten could exist.

And then, over a horizon line drenched in a perpetually greenish twilight, over a black sand shore covered with piles of harvested salt clumps and salt flats, his eyes faded from white to black for the last time.

chapter thirty two

Within the inner limits of Per.a, the throne of Anannke sat empty.

The nobles stared at it stupidly, waiting, none having any authority to even inquire where Necessity could possibly be. Insane plots to overthrow the dominion of the Anannke seeped through the thick walls of the compound.

Gossip.

Whispers that any Tryage unit could be given total dominion over the Empyrean via the abdication of the Anannke from the purification throne, finally able to define purity as the victor deigned fit, as well as its opposite, obliterating the three official states of perfected passage that safely ambled behind each council Head like obedient, protected sheep.

The de facto ability to punish all arrivals that did not live up to any newly christened parameters of cleanliness and call it purification resting within the hands of any one of the three Heads sent silent quakes of what was not allowed to be called Fear throughout the Empyrean on both sides of the Pe-ra complex walls.

The unspoken polite psychological war of three pathways that the Empyrean masses were conscripted into based on how they fared in and fell into the Empyrean from the bosom of the Anannke would regress into depravity erased from them prior to entry, leaving current inhabitants of the Emp useless and easily dominated by whatever was deified under new definitions as the Rightest Way.

All citizens under every councilor of the highest high were alarmed, without no spiritual vernacular to express it as such.

But when rumors that the bodhicitta paths ordained by the unspeakable ways of the Anannke were on the chopping block pushed through the Per.a purification complex's protective shell, alongside whispers that none of the nobles silently in allegiance with the necessities of current things in play were safe, only one mantra whispered at personal altars calmed any nerve.

"Fate rules."

All currently seeming to be benefiting were fearful that a date in this timeless place was on the horizon, one where the Fate that favored them would be overridden, and that the remnants of a faulty balance would finally be wiped out and replaced with something worse for all parties eternally present.

The spotty spiritual rap sheets obviously still smeared across the latest Citizens thresholding into the Empyrean in the midst of the reigning confusion grew in direct relation to the unspoken fears of all those enjoying the life after lives left in the realm. The dark vibrato of the escapades of those who had not yet ascended back into the Empyrean was even worse, their ministering powers perverting while trapped in hell on Earth assigned to charges. And the number of non- returns was so high that the Neobodhisattvas lined up to submerge in the spirit to be lights below panicked about setting out in the first place, no matter how intensively they had trained pre- assignment.

chapter thirty three

Artyo opened her eyes against a white-out that was starting to feel like the norm post-mortem and found herself seated lotus style. Chrome studs in black leather cushions pressed against her legs but her flesh felt nothing.

She shifted to bring her blue silk shrouded legs back to life. The side seams loosely laced up her hips and feather encrusted turquoise, green & orange silk aprons sat in her lap. Her half-cornrowed hair spilled wildly over her shoulders down to the small of her back. Her neck, chest and forearms were heavy with copper chains. Anger poured down from her heart and spiraled out of her limbs in search of him, only to find their hands already lazily entwined.

His bands were silver, his lips stained with what looked like oily blood. The bone structure that led her to him in the first place glinted as if he was made of gold while the hollows of his eyes and his cheeks had been darkened to the point of consumption. His Dominican braid of hair was unfurled down his back. Red slubbed silk trousers laced loosely up his hips, the triangular flashes of his honeyed flesh holding her attention. A grin spread over his face before he opened his kohl rimmed eyes as if he could feel hers.

It was the first time he'd ever seen her made up and from the expression on her face he knew she had no clue, which made him enjoy it all the more. Swirls of peacock blue, gold and green danced across her lids and something that glinted like what the Nefilim drank lined her eyes. She looked wet- every chiseled plane of her face played up. Her lips were flushed. He blushed at how beautiful she was always too stubborn to let herself be and wondered if he would have fought her as hard if she would have just looked how she did now in all those fucked up moments together behind them.

His off-kilter look made her self-conscious and she raised her fingertips up to her eyes, terrified of what was lodged there that had hypnotized him. Before Artyo could ruin the painstaking work, an old lady cleared her throat, scaring the shit out of them both. The two swiveled towards her, seeing her for the first time.

She sat cross-legged on a mountain of pillows and smiled as Artyo and Thyaz absorbed her. Layers of giant, embroidered silk kimonos worn as if slipped on after a bath were draped over her shoulders. Smeared down her exposed decolletage like war paint was what looked like liquid mercury. A different set of organs pushed themselves out of her pin-coated torso with every breath she took.Her brows stood out against the honeyed color of her skin and the brightness of the hair framing her face. Obscenely long, acid white ringlets hung in clumps around huge, gleaming white almond shaped eye sockets. The curls loosened as they dripped down and out across the mirror-like expanse of water they were all in like veins of the white-out that had pressed so coarsely against their eyes a blink ago. Her arms danced above her head as she cut a messy Mohawk into her hair. Tight, little black spirals stuck out all over her now exposed neck and ears. The clippings dissolved on the kimono and seeped into the fabric like India ink as they watched, gape-mouthed.

She looked like a salt and pepper-haired child playing dress up in her mother's clothes and ruining her hair with no adult supervision.

Roughly woven curtains of state marked out the receiving area they seemed in and shielded them from the pulsing white of the horizon beyond it as it shifted to a churning red and orange. The space around them seemed as if it were on fire due to the reflective liquid they floated in as the Anannke slid gingerly to its surface. Her kimonos sloshed into the chrome-colored water beneath feet that levitated obscenely atop it. She turned and slowly walked away from them, layers of red, green and blue silk billowing behind her as her hair wafted up towards the ceiling.

The Anannke turned halfway towards them and zoomed into their every detail in an instant. Thyaz's flesh twitched as he became nothing but a flash of cells flowing in different directions under it due to the press of the Anannke's orbs. Artyo stared after the Anannke like she was pornography in the purest sense of the word, unable to escape the heavy sense of déjà vu in the pit of her stomach keyed to Swiss cheese holes in her memory that ricocheted in her mind every time she blinked her eyes in disbelief. The two of them sat dumbfounded until she ordered them to follow her with a toss of her chin.

Thyaz elbowed Artyo, the Anannke's feet floating above the water amplifying any concepts of religion and contrition he had ever been exposed to. He protested Artyo's attempts to make him follow the Anannke first. The longer they took, the further Fate got away from them. The protective curtains of state moved with her, quickly exposing the two of them to the blinding glare of the red orb they were shocked to be beside. The heat sent the two scrambling into waters that rose up to their thymuses.

"It figures-" he muttered as the two began to trudge through whirling pools of waters behind the one who hadn't stopped to see if they were on her heels.

Artyo tried not to stare at the now seemingly mile-long strands of white hair floating from the Anannke's head as they settled on her shoulders like cobwebs and pulled both her and Thyaz in her wake. Their feet slipped across scarred marble underwater, the incline steeper with every step taken. The air burnt their lungs as they felt themselves sweat even under water. Artyo defiantly tried not to be mesmerized by the rainbows on small drops of sweat that rolled down her nose and splashed slow-motion into the silvery water. She wiped at her brow, freaked out by the metallic swirls of color that came off on her wrist. Looking down at the slowly receding reflective liquid now barely under their ribs she caught her first glimpse of what her core truly looked like and stopped in her tracks. She wiped furiously at the self she had spent so long trying not to be, streaking pretty bright pigments all over her hands with each swipe, only to watch in horror as the colors re-spread across her lids with a heavier hand, streaked like a Pollock painting. One hand crawled to her mouth in shock, the other towards Thyaz, who she missed by about a yard.

He was oblivious to the clouds of steam that danced off his body and silvery sweat that glinted on his exposed skin and in his hair like dew, enthralled by the curtains of state they had caught up to. He stopped and ran his hands across them, laughing as the fibers stuck to his fingers and stained them. Artyo stumbled forward and brushed her fingers against his shoulder blade, scattering the dew reflecting her true colors to her across his naked back. The blush-grin from before spread across his face. She looked like an angry, scared, exotic bird, streaks of color crawling up her forearms instead of feathers. He raised his newly stained fingers up to show her like a child, and she shyly grasped his wrist and pressed his palm into her face to calm her down. Thyaz burst out laughing at the sweetness in the gesture and they stood there, unaware of the water they were in evaporating at lightning speed.

He pulled her into him and wrapped his other arm around her, burrowing his head into the cloud of her joss stick scented hair unraveling in the atmosphere. She closed her eyes and listened to the blood gushing erratically inside his jugular as she wrapped her fingers into the downy hair at the nape of his neck. The fabric of their costumes suctioned to them, the copper and silver around their necks gleaming as if burnished. An eight-pointed star compass roughly cut into the traction-scarred marble bloomed below them, the last of the chrome-plated liquid pooling around them like klieg lights positioned in front of a world premiere marquee, putting their brazen, silent re-calibration of one another on display for all of the Empyrean to sector, if desired.

The Anannke's feet made contact with polished stones leading up out of the canal as she watched them comfort each other through herself, brow furrowed over their flouting any protocol the Anannke had become accustomed to as her minutes had swerved to eons within the realm. Memories tugged at the peripherals of her selective omniscience as she coughed against the taste of what used to register as blood flooding across the surface of her tongue. She cleared her throat to bring them back and burn the last remnants of life out of their optic nerves in preparation for the purification the complex she helmed specialized in.

Thyaz and Artyo felt the disconcerting, impatient press of the Anannke waiting and absently looked up. They scrambled clumsily up towards her timidly, hand in hand. The Anannke kept her back to them, looking out directly into the red orb. The sweetened scent of Nag Champa pulled their eyes away from each other and into an expanse of molten lava churning where the sky should have been. They shook as they stood gawking out into the streak of it.

The Anannke silently reveled, feeding off the appropriateness of their reaction. Below them, the Empyrean corkscrewed along the concave edges of the red star Thyaz suddenly realized they were somehow inside of and looking at as they stared out at its core.

The structures of the highest high braced onto both the
ascending and descending ridges of the inner skin of the star,
glinting like gigantic, fossilized scales smeared with streaks of
blood and dusted with gold. Metallic clusters gleamed in the
reddish light, wildly rising and falling the way chaotic
symphonies picked their way across the stained sheet music of
geniuses. The cocooned bridges seen off the inner balconies of
the Kagome-Arachne sector seemed dense and heavy
compared to everything seen now.

"Artyo- is this - is This is where you meant to -" Thyaz
stuttered softly, overwhelmed by the gloriously fiery vista
in front of them.

Hot tears poured down Artyo's cheeks as she dropped to her
knees. "…This can't be -"

The pressure within the processional ante-room they'd
traversed in the wake of the Anannke kept them from
falling away from the reality in front of them.

"No matter where you thought you were going ...This," the
Anannke hissed softly as she motioned to the expanse of
activity above and below, "Is what you have cast yourselves
into."

chapter thirty four

She picked at the long, curved pine needles stuck in the sweat on her calves after the first round. The sting of the scratches from crawling across them paled in comparison to the indigestion she felt on the other side of visions seen after the sky had opened and ripped her up into it.

She didn't know how long they'd stick. The visions. Never did. But the pathways activated by the blood streaming down her legs afterward would be with her forever if she had any say in it, no matter what came next.

She slid her soiled white tee shirt over her head and gingerly pressed the front of it to her left calf like she was doing a rubbing. Hunched over, she did the same thing on the back with her right calf, muttering to herself incoherently. The guides returned to the hallowed zone as she struggled back into it.

They knew she wasn't ready. That it wasn't time. According to their calculations. So they sat on their haunches along the creek that separated the holy ground she stood on from them. They peered down into the dust nervously.

The eldest guide sneaked a peek at her, sizing up the gore-streaked top. "Maybe it's already enough of a Letting-" he whispered conspiratorially, ready to return. Instantly, the earth below them shook violently and opened up, swallowing all but one of the guides like they were nothing more than an offering.

The last left guide cowered on his belly in the dust, crying like the neophyte he'd always known he was even before the litany of insults that were lobbed at him daily by his elders, afraid to look up and witness what only he'd been chosen as somehow pure enough to see.

She let out a blood-curdling scream. Bolting into action, the last guide's head snapped up and he lunged across the water a moment too late to catch her as she was roughly yanked back up into the sky.

He looked on in disbelief as giant, blood drenched humanoids materialized and surrounded her in the sky. They rotated slowly around her levitating body as the streaks of blood mapped out on her top and limbs spun out from her to them and danced in each of their palms. They peered intensely into the streams of blood that pooled in their respective hands as if they were ley lines in her, assigned to each of them. Intros and exits across space and time were calculated ambivalently before they callously dropped her cords like she was a forgotten maypole. They shot up into the sky as she plummeted back down and crashed in a heap at the feet of the bewildered last guide left.

He gently folded her into the nearby basket that he'd spent the duration of his pursuivantism preparing, covered it and apprehensively danced his acolyte hands through the appropriate blessings before he nervously eased the straps of it across his bony yet broad shoulders and lifted her, overwhelmed yet knowing he could lose his life if he forgot even one detail he'd witnessed since he'd been spared.

chapter thirty five

Hezuz came to in the shambles of his life that surrounded him.

Naked sycophants glided like flotsam on highs that he had bribed them with for company for so long that nothing was recalled before it.

He was haywire. Up had become down, backwards forwards, and whatever crossed his radar with any purity made him reek of a rot that he couldn't bear after comprehending the stench came from him but he'd just never noticed, so used to roosting in the glorified filth of his so-called success he'd been.

Hezuz dragged a crusty hand across bleary eyes and matted curls, depositing more crud on them than he wiped away. He startled a bit and stretched out his hand out in front of his face. It was coated with dried blood. The shock of it snapped him all the way awake as the flakes of blood slid into his eyes and joined the gunk rimming his irises as they readjusted to the darkness.

Scattered in piles around him were underage models with bruised legs, chests and faces, smeared with the shit and blood their agents had convinced them was their ticket to the big time, numbed out and drugged up. Comp cards stuck to filthy thighs to identify each of them at their highest highs. Their faces came back in flashes, memories that tortured his daytime so much that he had been high for decades to protect himself from the pain they inflicted regardless of him physically feeling anything or not. He was wracked with the recall of so many faces, clusters of fourteen year olds in the basements of ornate mansions playing spin the bottle in Mardi Gras masques with lecherously grinning men thirty years older and more that dangled introductions to the higher echelons of life in front of them like carrots.

Virginities were 'lost' time and time again to the delight of the pedophiles serviced, each child trying to outdo the one before her until it all dissolved into madness swirling around Hezuz like a violent storm that he stopped with a razor to his forearms, the only way out he knew.

He stumbled through piles of detritus in the dark, feeling his way up the stairs out of the hell built into the bowels of his own home. When he opened the door, brightness slashed him and brought him to his knees, making him literally crawl the last few paces out of his self made grave towards the light.

An inner garden glared at him across polished marble that felt like shards of glass under his knees as he inched towards it. It was only when Hezuz looked behind him that he noticed the parallel trails of blood that followed the path his wrists made. Bewildered, he looked down at old jagged scars that crawled up his wrists under tattoos of snakes that sat motionless except for the slow pulse of the veins in his arms. Suddenly they began to slither around his limbs. He hoarsely cried out and reached for the beautifully carved door handles he'd discovered in a Parisian flea-market lifetimes ago. The self-sacrilege down his wrists violently ripped back open upon contact and his life-force hurled itself out of him yet again. His head slammed down hard on the floor. "God-" Hezuz heaved, "Please...forgive me-in the name of-"

Hezuz tried to black out to no avail as the hyena-like laughter of the last one consciously sacrificed before it all forcibly became a blur echoed in his ears.

She stood over his almost emptied body, stunted more by the day it dawned on her that her parents had sold her to him as a child sex slave more than any twisted act he'd performed on her in the name of parentally sanctioned pedophilic predilection. She'd watched as, post-her parent's offering the nubile need continued to feast upon him and had gone crazy tracking underage food for the beast she'd seen as her ticket straight out of the hell her father had visited upon her elder sisters as their vain mother had looked away before it had reached her shore, into the big time of the luxurious ever-after with her prince, forever willing to throw increasingly younger girls than her to what she could no longer satisfy, no matter how small she viciously forced herself to stay to justify her visual worth to him and justify his dependence on her as his bottom bitch come child bride. It was the first time she could recall him actually getting the garden door open in his run, but it made no difference to her.

The demon child woman knelt over his bloodied body and inspected the gashes she'd watched him cut into his arms repeatedly to break away from the monster he had groomed her into. She sighed, ready to drink directly from them again, a just reward for what he'd turned her into, then froze as a soft wind swept in from outside across the bloody, sticky hairs on the forearm full of writhing snakes right before she made a grab for it.

A shower of downy, colorful feathers slowly floated between the demon Hezuz had groomed and his bloody body.

She inched back and squinted into the light of the garden that read as darkness to her. In a flash the demon saw a horrendous pile of blood-stained feathers thick with colors that violated her sight in this place with their purity. White eyes gleamed from within the center of them as the wings cradled his cracked open head, watching every move of the demon like it was plotting which vein would be ripped out of it first.

"Why don't you just let him go?!" the demon hissed as the angel chaotically spoke in tongues over Hezuz, each syllable making the craven beast flinch. The Angel continued to whisper over his body in four tonalities as the blood continued to flow from his wrists, turning almost black. "Look!! You- You're making him bleed more! You're doing my job for me!" the Demon screeched happily, licking her lips as the vestiges of her became more of the "it" she'd given herself to for nothing but revenge.

It laughed as blood crested from the base of his spine, roared up his body and flooded out of his arms and head.

"Told you we'd find you" the Angel whispered,"we've looked forever for you, through hells even worse than this one you built for you" the Herald growled. "That's it- watch- don't look away… don't look away from it- you need to see it for what it is, Malak- in the name of who, baby-" the Angel murmured in four tonalities as one. Hezuz's eyes weakly wobbled towards the demon.

"You're not helping him!" it cackled. "You're- you're helping me! Us! You're helping us! Do you think this was by chance? Do you think we hadn't planned this all along- We caught him and dragged him deeper as soon as he thought he'd gotten free! And we'll do it Again! And Again!Forever!" the demon crowed as roars of laughter boomed up from the basement below.

"Don't look away-" the Angel croaked into the broken crown of the head of Hezuz. "See it- See it for what it is- Then say it… so we never have to come back here again-" the Angel grunted authoritatively. The blood of Hezuz began to seep out of his pores and pooled around him as the demon screeched in delight at his feet. In the basement more demons howled as his blood began to drip down through the floorboards onto them.

"In the name of who-" the Herald whispered again. "You Did this- You made it out-On your very own- Just like I always told you that you would- that You'd open the door, yourself… and I'd be waiting- You're almost done -You know this-Now… In the name of who?" she hissed.

"You want him to die as badly as we do! You're making him bleed in hell!" the demon screamed from the center of the ruined woman-child as the minions ripped the basement to shreds below him, driven insane by the taste and smell of his spilled blood.

"Do you hear that? That's all that enabled him screaming out for their pounds of His Flesh, their liters of His blood- and you're helping make that blood flow- with that incessant… blathering! We Always make him fall- Every Time! There IS no escape! None!" The demon woman-child screamed, trying not to flinch at the flecks of foreign words pelting it that seemed to protect Hezuz from its touch. "You always were so stupid-" it seethed. "Stop muttering!" the demon crowed.

"In the name of who-" the Angel whispered again as Hezuz's eyes ran across the skins of the perdition popping into view that had chased him his entire life. Hezuz gagged on his own blood, roughly whipped his head up in the arms of the Angel and locked eyes as recognition of her slammed into his skull. Blood began to drain from his ears, mouth and nose. The residue rimming the irises of Hezuz shook, then disintegrated in puffs of reddish-black smoke that mushroomed in front of his eyes. A shock of strength exploded at the base of his spine and he sat up, the serpents hissing in alarm as they held on.

"Say it-" The Angel growled against his jugular, glaring at the demon who stepped back as the blood of Hezuz spread out around him like a lake that vibrated with each faint pulse of his body like he was its bass beat. The blood began to shift into letters along its edge, then words, promises scrawled in blood that could never be overturned, promises that had lived within Hezuz no matter the depths of hell he'd found himself in. He roughly flung the snakes off of him into the blood that devoured them as if it were acid.

"Say it- so I can do what I came here to do-" the Angel snarled.

The demon laughed nervously, unable to ignore the scriptures of consecration and dedication the blood letters formed as it dawned on it what the Angel was doing.

"WAIT! You- You're bleeding him out?! You can't Do that!!" the demon screeched. "No! No! You can't- That's not how this-No!!"

"Jesus! God-forgive me in the name of Jesus!" Hezuz choked as the last few drops of his infected blood pushed out until only the remnant blood Hezuz had received in faith as a small boy remained. Everything around Hezuz howled as the Angel that cradled him began to laugh darkly.

Weak relief spread across him as he strained to look up at the Herald through his matted, bloody hair. The spirit of Hezuz flat-lined, locked onto the gaze of his demented Angel, his soul burnt from the inside out, leaving nothing more than a shell of purified ash and spirit in his Angel's lap as his captives wailed below him and the beast at his feet.

The Herald stopped laughing, looked down at the shell of her charge, then up.

In a flash the spirit in the shell shot up into the sky above the garden, free. The principality he had been imprisoned in for an eternity shook from the velocity of his escape.

chapter thirty six

The vastness of the empty mansion come prison echoed around the Angel crouched over the husk of Hezuz. The dust from his corpse mingled in the thick air with tears that something higher wicked away as they attempted to fall.

"How could you!?" The demon howled petulantly. "You saved him?! You KNOW what he did- to me! To ME!" she cried out, morphing back into the body of the thirteen year old child she had been when this madness began. "It's not fair! I – I was owed revenge forever for what he did to me! It was to be FOREVER!"

"And you interfered!" the demon in her screeched.

"You're right, you were-" the Herald said calmly, "but Forever just ended."

"And you-" a red winged Herald growled as it stepped away from the pile of technicolor feathers it had been hidden within, "You *technically* exchanged your right to revenge by going in with the Light-bringer that is trying to escape the consequences of His actions even as you speak, and leave you to pay for it all."

Two tiered Harbinger Angels with vivid green wings rose from under the wings of the first and blocked the Light-bringer trying to fade away back into shadows. "HE is who we're here for," the smaller of the two green Angels purred. "And who- if you had only listened, you would understand is the true architect of the hell you chose to try to rule in, not Hezuz-"

"...Now You- you have a choice-" the Blue winged Herald murmured,"Forgive the unfathomable things done to you so that the unspeakable things that you have done to the children YOU pulled into this pit like a crab in a barrel after you… can be forgiven… and walk the road your decision to do that built out, with grace and eternal protection until-"

"NO!"
"-Or-"
"I said No! I won't!" the woman-child snarled," why bother telling me the alternative?!"
"OR-" the first Herald snarled again.
"Or what?! Stay here with Him?!" the woman-child snarled, motioning towards the Light-bringer pinned behind the two scythes of the green winged Heralds. "The only one who ever tried to make sense of Any of this?!- This is what I know! This is the best my mother said I would ever get! Her mother gave her up the same way to my dad- it's how it's-Done! It's the way where I'm from! You just get married Off early! If you're Lucky!" she spat angrily.

"Do you FEEL lucky having gone through-" the youngest of the green Heralds asked coldly. "Did living through that shit again and again Ever …feel like fucking luck?!"

The woman-child spat again as something in her fought against herself. She viciously shoved it down.
"Didn't fucking look like Luck from where I am standing-" the Herald, continued, exhausted by the hunt and outraged at the insolence.

" You know What?! That's right!" the woman child snarled nastily. "Looked like to you! Because all your kind usually does is stand there and Watch! How dare you past judgment on what I have done when your kind usually only is in it for the show, just like those lecherous fucks this circus gets put on for! Fuck your judgment of the Hell you WATCHED me find a fucking way through! Fuck your opinion of ANY camaraderie between me and Any demon who showed up and at least fucking DID something in the absence around me due to your kind!" she roared. "You want me to pray to God after all this?! I know who my allegiance is to! The demons who at least walked through the hell you watched me in With me! I'm staying here! With him!" she shrieked and pointed at the Light-bringer.

The ancient red winged Herald opened her mouth, closed it, then muttered, "No."

"It's not even worth it, Meroe-" the elder green Harbinger whispered.

"No, yes it…is-" the crone replied simply as she turned to the woman-child and dropped every vestige of humanity she'd adorned herself with out of respect of the process in the hunt. The mansion buckled due to the shift in the atmosphere.
"See, part of *your*.. Kind's issue…is that you…fucked around with darkness for so long, consciously, almost erotically

that…you lost every gauge of the clarity of spirit you were ever endowed with," she murmured.

"Have you seen anything like this before? Have you?!"Meroe barked at the woman child who quaked before her in her natural state.

"Of course not! Too busy playing with your tarot cards, playing sexy, sado-masochistic witches, acting like you liked all the shitty things that happened to you because you were too much of a coward as an adult to face that you didn't!" she huffed. " *My* kind? Generations of *your kind* couldn't deal with the truth that Your fucking selfish parents WERE fucking Monsters! They were assholes who sacrificed your psyche for baubles, brand names and social standing! You were raised by sickos more at ease with the idea of you being fucked in the head your entire overtly sexualized life- as long as they profited from it- than the idea of stopping the adults- in house and otherwise- from fucking with you up due to the gifts those other adults gave them."

Meroe seethed. "So you hate US?! The ones you can feel there with their hands fucking tied! Instead of the fucking parents who set you up in this shit?!YOU called your fucked up mother all the time while you lived in this mansion! Hoping ONE day she might just maybe cry out against whatever depravity she'd sold you into! And what did she do with every one of those calls YOU made in?! Acted jealous because your house was bigger than hers, and bragged about all the shit the man who'd denigrated you to the point of you crying out To her had recently shipped to her in thanks for the gift of you! You spend lifetimes hating us who you can't see because you refuse to have the balls to hate the ones you fully see destroying you- And fuck taking that rap anymore!"

"Look at me!" the uncloaked Herald roared. "-ANY one of *my kind* who…watched you go through hell was ignored every step of your way towards it! Anything not keyed to the bullshit leading you deeper INTO the bullshit you picked up instead of what we called you to is not heard until You want to hear-"

The elder green Herald walked over the help Meroe regather her countenance as the elder angel heaved angrily.

"The answer is still NO," the woman child barked apathetically. "He was still there for me more than any-"

"Fine-only..." the elder green Herald smiled.
"Only what?" the demon in the adult woman who had just declared her choice to remain in hell snapped.
"He won't be here."
"What?!"

A strange breeze danced in from the open garden door. The two green tiered Heralds that were almost the spitting image of each other turned and firebombed the Light-bringer as the woman-child watched in horror, then shot up into the sky with him strung between the two of them.

The demented blue Herald looked at the demon the woman-child had chosen to become, once in ignorance and now in seething, dysfunctional wisdom. She had never given up on the freedom the Red Herald had long ago seeded Hezuz with. "Go to your son, Meroe -he needs you."

Meroe looked at Amybalis as the understanding of all unsaid things passed between them.

"Are you sure?"the Eldest Herald asked as the wings of Amybalis shimmered in the hallowed garden light.

"Yes. You know what they want him for. You're the only way he's going to make it through without capsizing." Amybalis murmured. "Besides... this one...is one of mine-" the Blue Herald chuffed to her elder.

Meroe slammed up into the higher atmospheres of hell, leaving Amybalis nose to nose with the newly christened DBC, a Demon by Choice that had once been an unprotected, glaringly forsaken child.

"You should have just left him to me!" the now official demon hissed at her.
"He wasn't mine to leave, Meadhbh." she said simply.
Amybalis's blue wings peppered with red and green stretched out behind her as she cocked her head to the side and peered into the remnant of the soul that had let this last life run roughshod over it as the DBC imagined ripping the Angel's wings off.

"What? Oh! You want my wings? Think it will help? Here." Amybalis pulled out her acurved blade, violently sawed her wings off and roughly threw them on the ground at the feet of the DBC. An enraged yet terrified Meadhbh stepped back.
"Now...what?" the Head Herald growled.

"I'm not forgiving him-" Meadhbh snarled and stepped back again. Things slammed into the frame of the basement door a few paces behind her. She jumped forward and almost tripped over the hacked off wings.

Amybalis sighed. "Too bad... Maybe They… the ones you willfully pulled into this to feed him and yet still act like you were just solely a victim, stand here with utterly no remorse or repentance over betraying... will eventually be more forgiving of you than you were able to be-"

The floor shook as the devils in the basement below banged against the floor. "You always wanted dominion of this god-forsaken manse. Hope the feathers help," Amybalis whispered, "beyond the tar." She stepped across the threshold into the garden and started to shut the door, then stopped. "When you're ready to forgive him and want to get home, open the door. If you can make it to it."

" I just waited out forever for you to give him the chance to. Hopefully you will fare better, faster with yours than he did with you."

Meadhbh rolled her eyes. "What else?"
"Enjoy dominion. No co-rulers, even." Amybalis whispered.

Meadhbh rolled her eyes again then jumped as the basement door creaked under the force of the rage on the other side of it. She whirled around to look at it shake in its moorings.

"Hope you really are as much a "demon" as you've convinced yourself that you are...you're certainly about to find out either way-" Amybalis whispered.

The gentlest click of the garden doors latching echoed in the space. Everything went quiet.

Meadhbh looked around at the mansion she'd always fumed was rightfully hers for all that she'd been subjected to. Anger, pride and fear fought across her countenance as all that had been nurtured under the floorboards of the mansion exploded into dominion all the way up to the rafters, tearing Meadhbh limb from limb in the process.

When she came to, she was in the body of a child coated in tears and chicken feathers as her favorite pet was sacrificed for the ritual by her mother and aunts, teetering on the verge of the first of many choices she'd live out again and again in hell, forever reloaded for her until she chose to choose differently.

chapter thirty seven

Sector, the atmospheric communications system permeating the space, picked their fields of energy for the questions they were too stunned to formulate as the Anannke stared forward.

The decorum shown by Necessity was opaque, brittle. Required. Especially in consideration of how their presence flouted every protocol the Empyrean was built upon.

"They have indeed synchronized enough to be suitable, dare I say even viable for roads that must be de facto walked in the fiery abode of the-" Sector mused against the internal ear of the Anannke. *"Surprisingly, stunningly viable -"*

The Anannke choked on Sector's report, the thinly veiled outrage at one she'd long since handled somehow audaciously within her hive on full display across the surface of her if anyone had dared to look. Her hair defensively frothed around her like a toric scrim that parts of her screeched in, within full sight of others yet somehow not ever seen, violent storms she sporadically found herself strung up in that would have made no sense to any who had been accepted into her Highness's court, hidden from not only them but also from herself. She thrashed around in tangled bubbles of incoherent thought, strangled and suffocated, screaming for a help that Necessity never was privy to.

Coins frothed out of her mouth and spun in the biosphere of follicular torment. She writhed and choked less than a yard and a half from the uninvited on their knees at the cusp of her realm, yet not even the faintest disturbance within and around her Highness registered to them.

The Anannke wildly grabbed for the crossed coins, roughly flipping each one down the back of her long fingers into their purse, the ordered count calming whatever was astray until she could step back into the aspect of herself that she had floated away from and re-engage with the impossibilities that knelt before her. She thought of weaving, of harps, of order and counted off the the literal necessities for life keyed to each cool coin ritualistically slid into the bag, then paused, an item still left on that hallowed, calming list with naan a crossing coin to be found to key it to. The inability to finalize the count, the incompletion of the self-soothing compulsion slid a whole other mask into place.

One of remembrance, comprehension...and wrath.

The toric scrim dropped.

Artyo and Thyaz turned towards her, utterly dazed by the magnetic magnificence before them, unable to see her narrowed white orbs. The Anannke turned on her heels and floated down the walkway, unable to fathom not being followed.

chapter thirty eight

The terrace they had been introduced to the realm on wrapped around the outer limits of the glass enclosed House of Gold- the Pera Purification complex. The walkway emptied into a series of open-air courtyards that eventually led to the heart of the complex. The spigot and drain system they had encountered upon arrival was the closest thing to inner windows and doors in walls.

Splashes of gold were everywhere, barefoot prints glistened across the woods and polished stone. Globules of gold floated defiantly in quicksilver streams that churned past in low-slung partial walls, delineating where the outdoors ended and the inner work began as if the reality of running water was an art in and of itself.

The trains of the silk robes of the Anannke fluttered around Artyo's head like banners, color-coding each and every area she was being deemed privy to see. Churning red skies glinted off of huge toppled granite obelisks dragged from realms even the ancients of days would be hard pressed to remember, marking the inner sanctums of huge open spaces. Toddler bodhisattvas dressed in royal blue lay sprawled on padded mats, knocked out after ambrosia. Gigantic statues of god and man vandalized eons ago lay overturned and tattooed with graffiti in the courtyards. Red-swaddled already Elohim infants gurgled in pairs on pillows in the shade of the idols. What looked like copper veining began to appear and progress towards smears of minerals against the glassy outer membrane. Beyond that, children dressed in green that were the size of second graders sat lotus style on piles of leaves spread across slabs of sandstone along a churning silver babbling brook. The threesome cut through the courtyard keyed to green, Thyaz as oblivious to everything as Artyo was spooked by it, unable to look away from the doughy looks on the faces of the children as she passed and soft syllables from their hooded habit wearing gurus that mingled with the sounds of flash-flooding water.

The Anannke took note of both responses with a twitch of the vein between her two front teeth. The snatches of red sky overhead became fewer and farther between, replaced by mesh and sheets of metal bolted into place with gigantic rivets that gleamed golden against the pinkish copper.

The Anannke cleared her throat. "This is my territory. I am not God as you have been domesticated like goats to know of and abhor ...but I govern all that falls under the aspects of what you would call as such. Everything you need to concern yourself with regarding existence sprung from my head as a river of Necessity. In a sense, the threads that dance through this atmosphere you are so captivated by are all that ever was and will ever be allowed to continue to be-"

"But-" Artyo started, flustered.
"Niet!!!-" the Anannke barked without moving her lips.

They slammed their hands over their ears and pressed against each other, shielding themselves from the sonic blow of the sound. Blood trickled through their fingers and dried instantly into red snowflakes that fluttered away from their ruptured ears. The Anannke turned on her heels inside of herself, sliced through her own freeze frame and glared down at them.

"To ask you why you are here is a moot point." she seethed as they cowered. "I know why you're here. You don't even have a clue of the glorious artillery you were designed to be, so your escape velocity is of no import," she said dismissively to a frozen Thyaz. She took Artyo's near-catatonic chin in the palm of her lineless hand.

"And you..." she whispered as she shifted the muscles in Artyo's still shocked face until they were looking each other in the eye, " you have had the audacity to Have actually found a way to come...here... to eradicate... The Necessity of all things? hmm. ha. hmph. Ha~" The darkest smile spread over the partially blackened lips of the Anannke as she chuckled. " And YOU...stole from me to do it..." she snarled softly, " and...Maybe that is why you were allowed to die… so melodramatically. Ha. A tad early. Interesting rewrite. I must admit I couldn't have scripted that glorious end for you better myself. Ah well."

She dropped a still mesmerized Artyo's chin disinterestedly and slid back through herself as if caught up in a dance while standing still. The secondary frozen image of the Anannke still staring stoically ahead exploded into billions of balls of light that boomeranged back into the surface of the now freely floating being.

The Anannke raised her left brow one quartered section at a time, an exquisitely arched centipede slashed above the glaring orbs befit a god. "But by leapfrogging as you have done, you can't have but the slightest clue beyond fallacies and fantasies-that had to be erroneously believed in order to cross in the first place. You are a fluke that I must fix,"the Anannke hissed, "You've made your escape velocity, no matter its potency, nothing but a lie that will fall on you like a house of cards, sans instruction." she purred. "So instruct you, for the benefit of all within the realm that you have broken into, I shall."

Artyo and Thyaz suffered through violent fits without any assistance as the Anannke flickered in and out of sight in front of them. Artyo's spine shot up from the floor and bent back towards it awkwardly in an unnatural bell curve, her skull stopped from slamming back into the ground by Thyaz's twitching thigh. The Anannke floated back over to the two of them.

"You overshot-" the Anannke said mildly, finding words banal enough for them to make sense of what they'd done. Hordes of butterflies splattered with reds, blues and greens fluttered out of her mouth like vomit as she prattled on beatifically. The syllables danced in the air around the two of them on the floor, the beating of their wings soothing their scorched sensory systems as chunks of rhetoric seeped in."Systematically satisfied pursuit … abundance...no concept to dig...posterity-fathom the deeper things true immortality do...the trivial for them to register… materialistic fluff ...breadth and width … wildest dreams...Called prosperity... meant... springboards of broader eternities "God"…blasphemed ... artifice as ultimate power. End all. Be all," the Anannke drawled. "And so it was. Just not in the way minds below imagined it would be-" Abysmal irises rose up in the white orbs of the Anannke, a show of kindness towards them, a reminder of the physical they'd so recently known.

Thyaz felt the words of the Anannke pry through his temples as understanding slowly seeped into areas of his brain he'd never bothered to use on Earth. He was hooked.

"What has been ...accomplished ...by you apart but somehow as one, sans full genomic script revelation, no less, is beyond extraordinary- In the past, those who have aimed for Ascension got no farther than there," the Anannke continued as she motioned towards the pulsating realm below them.

"Transfixed by the entry hit of bliss like Earth's addicts, a deluge of them came, mucus clogging the works, walking into the dawning of selfish prayers sent up in earnest and answered. A mockery, really...too much sudden faith in supposedly impossible things sprung up as if all else on the road to where they were scheduled to go was eradicated on sight... It was an onslaught of sniveling emptiness, posturing for the best without realizing that their definitions of it were shallow… The highest attainable high was suddenly Nirvana *For one and for all*, like…" the Anannke searched for a feasible metaphor. "Like a nightclub past its prime, clogged by the braying of Bridge and Tunnel trash. This went on for so long that a predisposition for the spectacular and miraculous vanished. Entry into the highest high suddenly had the prerequisite of the equivalent of a spiritual tic-bath and a plastic surgery stint to weed out topical imperfections that would remind your kind of whence they came." "Now, penance was still on offer for those who banked on it being integral in the afterlife as pomp and circumstance, orchestrated perfectly for souls programmed to never look deeper than the things positioned around them. As they say, Give the people …what they want." The Anannke drawled.

"Fate is in the hair- these strands are all that has ever been. The fate you individually create is mapped out in your hair. The longer your hair, the longer you are bound by what happened to you as it grew. Cut it off, you release all that energy."

The prattling of Fate bounced off of Artyo's mainframe ambivalently as Thyaz soaked up the words of the Anannke like a parched sponge. He used everything in him to force himself to speak through the mind-grip they were in the midst of. Thyaz suddenly whispered, completely lucid in the intense download of information. "Then... why were you cutting off all the black hair instead of the old white hair when we first came to, here?"

The white hair on her head cascaded down and draped itself all over, glinting like rivulets of spring water in the sun. Sector silently re-routed Thyaz's vision, hyper-extending it against his will. His eyes forcefully locked in on strand after chopped strand of hair across the head of the Anannke as one after another of the black hairs bowed. Sector compressed the imagery as it erupted like the orgasm a whore kept sleeping around in search of. Thyaz stuttered under his breath, rocked, both fused to and forcibly ripped apart from the shocked anima in his lap. His body vibrated like a struck tuning fork.

"The older ones are more apt to accept ...how things *must* go. As long as their fears are energetically fed, etcetera, etceteras," the Anannke murmured. "Come- much is to be attended to."

chapter thirty nine

The buzzing in Artyo's ears and a past that had been all but burnt off with the ferocity of her crossing and the inability to place what she was vibrating to pulled her out of the shock the first view of the Empyrean had triggered.

The dissonance in her ears grew louder and her steps smaller the farther they went. Something in the air reminded her of honey.

Artyo stopped and looked around. The large mesh to her right was hexagonal, bolted into the walls of the hall they were proceeding down. The sounds of whimpering grew louder. She leaned in, sure the sound was coming from somewhere behind it. Her fingers danced inches away from the gold-spun net, hesitant.

The cackle of a woman sliced through the air around her, making her trip backwards and then forward as she fell through the wall and disappeared.

chapter forty

Loud and chaotic, the white-out returned, devouring the copper drenching Artyo's and licking noisily at the makeup that had festively adorned her. The aprons and edges of the fabric her lower body had been festooned with disintegrated.The sounds of shrieks and catty laughter boomeranged in the air around her as the white space pulsed with the energies of forgotten women on holiday in hell with one another.

"...You needed to put that child out of her misery-"

"I am surprised you decided to take on the challenge of it-"

"Having That in your house-"

"That child of his he infested you with-"

"Brought into this world destined to be a whore!"

"Well, no matter- we showed her-"

"It was good to find that we were okay-"

"Yes! At least we could still have that communion-"

"Victory never tasted so sweet-"

"The best flavor is in the marrow of a broken, small bone-"

"And in the end, we all still have each other-"

"That's right! Sisters!"

"Forever!"

The cluster of dead women appeared.

Zombies. Crouched low in ashes, faded skirts tossed up over hips, legs spread wide to show both sets of bloodied lips housed in them. No matter what color they used to be, everything was now shrunken or bloated and gray, bruised by never-ending nights fighting with women just like the backstabbing minions they had decided to be when they'd had a conscious choice to do better on Earth.

They preened as they sucked on relic bones of broken children for marrow, for the temporary color each fresh hit brought to their lips, reminding them of their higher selves in spite of the gnarled fingers and matted hair slicked to their scalps in this afterlife.

One inhaled as if she could smell fresh meat in the air for real.

The scent of it caused a flush of color that had previously only infected her sucking mouth to rise up and spread across her forehead until the beauty she once was reverberated in the space.

Her cohorts looked up and screamed , enraged. They swarmed her, tackling her to the ground before she could speak on the scent that had enlivened her. They howled as they cannibalized the member of their own crew, each screaming for the life that had somehow been inhaled momentarily by her.

"LIFE! Here!? In you this whole time?!"

Aghast, Artyo watched as the pile of swarming ratwomen feasted. They became grayer than before due to consuming the death they already were. They gagged due to the taste of themselves being swallowed whole and began to retch.

They puked, unable to stomach the meat of what they truly were, vomiting on each other again and again until the place seemed about to explode, the smell of their stomach acid mixed with the scent of old Florida water and spoiled raw chicken thick in the atmosphere.

Artyo kicked the imagery away as she crawled backward before she was seen.

They looked up in unison, wiping the vomit from their mouths into their hair as they cracked the rigor-mortised muscles in their livor-mortised limbs. "No!" one whispered in disbelief.

"It can't be-" another cried out as she started to shuffle slowly towards Artyo.

"Her?! Here?! In Our paradise?!" yet another screamed as she backed away, remembering.

Harsh laughter erupted again, eating at Artyo's skin like the acidic saliva on the tongues they licked at the regurgitated chunks of dead flesh smeared across their faces with. A few moved towards her, wailing comfort to their sisters as they did.

"Don't be afraid! She's Life!"

"She's come to bring us more Life!!"

Artyo jumped to her feet and ran backwards, then tripped over thin air.

chapter forty one

Artyo shook her head, unable to process what she'd just seen. The terrors evaporated as her bottom connected with the floor beyond the mesh. Wild-eyed, bruised and nearly naked, she looked after the Anannke as she sprinted forward, shrugging herself out of the spirals of colored silk that had encased her shoulder blades that then floated upwards into the hair that trailed above and behind her along the copper ceiling, slowly dissolving back into the essence of her.

The quickly-growing black coils around the Anannke's nape and ears glinted in the darkened pinkish light of the space the Anannke slashed through, lit from within. Her mercury smeared exposed skin left trails in the air as if every glance was a snapshot, the concept of Fate itself as the penultimate mirage. Thyaz ran after the blur as if Artyo never existed, Fate his only guide.

Mistrust that had been cut down in the bowels of heaven sprouted wings that flapped against Artyo's eyes violently. The buzzing noises re-introduced themselves into the space that sprung up between them.

Artyo took a few steps forward before the sound of static pulled her back in the direction she had just come from, avoiding the clumped trails of white hair streaming along the floor and ceiling. A strange sensation bloomed in her body in slow motion, rolling through her in reverse. For every arm that swooshed down through the air as if underwater, an opposing leg curved, foot bent up towards it, lost in it, flooded by memories of Shiva dancing the universe towards destruction and order. The mesh panels along the hallway began to pulse . Her eyes closed as she slowly lifted up off the ground on tiptoe as she arched backwards until both feet levitated completely off the floor. The chambers along the hall vibrated as her body spun in it. Her eyes fluttered back open.

A being cloaked like Death on Earth itself covertly made its way out of one of the cells. Artyo gasped. All that was hidden behind the mesh inhaled and exhaled greedily in response.

Surprised, the Reaper robed being turned around, grabbed Artyo by the throat and lifted her up, peering into her face. Terrified, Artyo's eyes slammed shut so as not to see what had to have been Death itself. She felt the sinews in her neck going limp with gut-wrenching fear. A slow smile of recognition rose up in the features of the face under the hood of the cloak. It looked up towards where the red sky would be if they were not so deep within the complex.

"Irony. But good timing." It whispered telepathically.

Artyo's eyes fought against an attempt to spring open in shock. "Wh-what-?" she stuttered inside of herself. "No- Please-!"

"No. I want you to see what you have set off. Firsthand," It growled, then slammed its' palm over Artyo's third eye with such force that the reaper hood shifted backwards, fully revealing the terrifying beauty of Third Head of council's visage.

Artyo's eyes ripped all the way open, fully loaded with all what was left of her human mainframe could bear. The chamber Third had come out of whirled back into place around her imprint, counter-point successfully loaded. Third roughly tossed Artyo beside nearby mesh like a crumpled bag. It re-cloaked and covertly left the calibration zone of Per.a that it's oft- chided feminine mystique quietly gave at-will access to, unbeknownst to the rest of the Tryage council preparing for war.

Unconscious, Artyo lay in an awkward heap, face bashed in, silvery foam dribbling from her mouth. Sickening streams of red and white refracted against the ceiling as all the absorbed chrome tinged waters she'd trudged through leeched out onto the floor. A guttural, cannibalistic gasp erupted on the far side of the honeycomb mesh as if it could smell her. The sharp inhalation was followed by a high- pitched wail that seemed to turn in on itself trying to magnetically drag her body towards it through the veil it couldn't cross.

Her body became buoyant in the liquid and shifted on the surface of the pool of all that had poured out of her. The mesh crackled as her fingertips slid towards it. The high pitched wail ricocheted around the hall as the rest of her was pulled across the threshold. The quicksilver that had flooded out of her encased her like an amniotic sac as she disappeared.

chapter forty two

The sac slid through the darkness that loomed on the other side of the mesh, pulled deeper and deeper by gravity until the quicksilver poured into a small stream trickling through the bottom of a stalagmite and stalactite crammed cavern.

Artyo's unconscious form dead-man floated face down deeper into the tunnel system. Stalagmites glowed green, gray and blue under the surface of the murky, shimmering waters as small bubbles trailed out of her nose and broke on the surface with more and more ferocity, disturbing the currents of the stream. They began to softly whirlpool under her until she was pulled down and spat back up on her back. Face up, the colors in the cave shifted from green and gray to reds, ochres and pinks that glinted in the dark. The bruises on her broken face glowed burgundy in the half light as her body was pulled towards the rough hewn throne on the shore of an inner sea.

The qilin on the coast lost their minds, panting in response to the surprise scent of freshly felled flesh not having been a dream. Who the beasts belonged to chuckled darkly on the throne as they went delirious with desire on the shore.

His chalky white, many- breasted mantle lay open to expose the hair shirt of dreadlocks whose hem pooled at the semblance he had of feet and pressed against the closest thing that he had to flesh. The surface of him was nothing but a dense, deep, undulating shadow, simultaneously an absence of light even as scatterings of it seemed to dance across what could be seen of him like stars. His head lolled back as he opened his eyes languidly. The buds in the crown of thorns he wore burst into bloom and the scent of roses filled the cave complex.

He floated over to the edge of the waters to get a better look, wrapping obscenely long fingers around the double scope bolted to the shore. Lashes that seemed to go on forever undulated up into the thick atmosphere around him from the far rim of the scope as if tasting everything around them. There was no expression on his face, only inexplicable darkness as he raised his hand and pressed it towards the form floating in the water.

The body stopped and bobbed up and down in place. The qilin screamed as they ran around him in circles, pleading for permission to retrieve it as he floated back down onto his throne like the beleaguered ruler he was, the darkness wrapped around him pulsing with the desire of the qilin. Resigned, he looked out at her corpse, then down at his unlined, pitch black and blue hands, knowing that they were filthy with why this shell had somehow made its way to his shore in the first place, no matter whether or not any would ever accuse him and all he had dominion over of it. He stretched out his hands over the waters and magnetically pulled her to the shore as his feral pets went wild. Full of disdain, with a toss of a hand he sent the qilin splashing into the mercury laden waters to retrieve the bones.

The pack fought each other as two of their jaws slammed down into her somehow still breathing but dead flesh and dragged her to the shore. They spat her at the foot of their beloved's throne, waiting for permission to eat.

The darkness in him stroked their horns, knowing they were famished for fresh meat. He rose up and gestured towards the water and they went mad, seeing their favorite bird to prey upon float down onto the surface of the calm sea, baiting them. They howled and charged it, no longer interested in the fresh dead flesh they'd brought to him.

The cover of darkness he lived as below absently wrapped its long fingers around Artyo's ankles like the shot deer she was to him and dragged her through the black sandy loam of the shore deeper into the cavern system. Her body thunked against low-lying circular basalt stone altars full of various offerings of tangled hair and cocoons until they'd arrived at the circular stone platform right outside of his lair.

The darkness in him dissipated as he bent down to lift her bruised and half-drowned body up onto it, his many breasted cloak falling away to expose wings caged by his hair shirt as he sat down on the edge of the altar and peered into her broken face.

Streams of quicksilver danced across her like a tangled net dress. Her meridians had been dislodged from the depths of her body and careened against the outermost membrane of her due to the trauma she'd gone through to get there.

"I should've never okayed the clipping of your wings. It made you too vulnerable to the atrocious things they had in store-" he grunted as he tugged off the hair shirt he'd worn forever under his mantel of abundance trying to atone for his biggest failure. Angry and repentant, his own wings burst forth and glimmered in the darkness of the cave.

"First lets cut you out of all this," he growled and ran his hands an inch above her skin. The gnarled net of meridians slashed through the surface of her skin and evaporated.

Artyo came to with a start, choking on water still in her lungs.

She drew back in horror at the cloaked cloud of darkness hovering over her as he dragged his weathered, dark, shimmering hand across her destroyed face to calm her, healing it in the process.

The space around them became flooded with the smell of the buds blooming again in the crown of thorns he wore as petals from the first bloom fell on her in consecration. She peered where his face should have been, seeing only the density of the darkest night as he took the hand he'd healed her with and dragged it up to his face from his sternum, exposing a human form that she'd be able to process from his head to his heart. His readjusted eyes flooded with silent tears as Artyo shakily reached out her hand and stroked the face of the only beginning and end she'd ever truly known and passed back out.

chapter forty three

He carried her to the spindles, working quickly. He gingerly wove a cocoon of blanked tussah silkstrands across her unconscious form on the standing altar.

His hands slid in and out of her body as he filled every orifice in her that had been depleted upon arrival. His gnarled fingers danced as he corrupted the cach encoding programmed into her pathways before time. Her body pulsed, trying to reject the maker's hack to no avail. As he slid the last filament of silk up against her pineal gland his beast of beasts groaned laboriously from deep within his lair, causing him to look up.

He knew he didn't have much time.

Finally finished, he spirited her away himself, qilin at his heels.

He left the shore and the beasts fell silent as he rose up above the waters with her newly gowned form draped heavily in his arms. He looked up in repentance and then down at her face for the last time. The new netting she was encased in pulsed and seeped into her skin.

The cloud of darkness that he was glinted in the half light of the cave as they plummeted deep into the inner waters.

The ancient one that was the God of love before Time regulated it to no more than a sector slid through the waters of his realm into the river on the edge of places unable to bear the reality of his imprint anymore, a re-woven Artyo in his arms.

He deposited her nakedly redressed form on the edge of almost forgotten shores, knowing it was best not to look around before he roughly shoved her through the protective mesh and out onto the copper floors of the hive before sinking back down into them as she slowly came to.

chapter forty four

The qilin, slick with the blood of their sacrifice wrestled their way back to Sector's altar in his absence.

The bad one with a little good noticed the tangle left on the altar from Artyo's quicksilver webbed dress and, due to the little bit of good inside of it, admonished itself and looked away.

"What are you staring at?" the Good with a little bad asked accusingly.
"Nothing," the Bad mumbled and pawed his partner in its fiery head. The wrestling continued until the Good saw the tangle.

"I can't believe you! You know we aren't allowed!"
"I didn't DO anything!" the Bad fussed back.

Lost in his thoughts, Sector returned and separated the two qilin as the Good ratted out the Bad. Sector silently dragged the Bad away.

The Good preened sanctimoniously and, as soon as Sector was out of ear shot, pounced on the tangle and got caught up in it.

The qilin howled in pain as the web cut into its flesh,liquified and started to soaked into it. His body began to turn to ash from his tail up due to the war of the tangled against the inner constitution of the qilin. He transmogrified into a quivering male form.

The female qilin charged in and howled in pain as she watched him as he shape-shifted against his will. Sector showed up right before the shift reached his Qilin's ribcage.

"Tsk, tsk. Told you not to..." Sector sighed, "mess with this-" he deftly slid his fingers across the qilin's skin and the quicksilver solidified, magnetized to its maker's touch. Sector ripped the tangle choking the qilin off of his neck, the shapeshift stopped just in time. He stroked the last tuft of qilin coat on the terrified beast's chest. The qilin flinched in fear as the blackened shadows where the rest of him used to be solidified into the form of a kouros crowned by a qilin head. He cowered and then shrieked when he drew himself into a ball and recognized he had human limbs. He opened his mouth to roar like an animal. "What the-" he screamed in shock.

His partner yelped and dove under the nearest altar. His hooves flew to his face as they morphed into hands. He stared on in shock, then looked up at Sector's glinting face in the half-light.

"Re'em, come!" Sector barked. Whimpering, the 2nd qilin approached and sniffed him, curious. She perked up and licked his qilin face, then burrowed into his human lap.

"It's still Rimu," Sector whispered as he stroked both Re'em & Rimu.

"It's okay, You're still Rimu." Sector grabbed Rimu by the ears and pulled his furry muzzle towards him, gently pressing his 3rd eye to the base of Rimu's horn. "But now you see why I forbade you, don't you?" Rimu moaned sullenly. "It's okay. Live in it a little while. You may decide you like this form better."

Sector took the tangle and left the two qilin curled up around each other.

He traipsed past the repositories for what the tangles distilled down to under the hidden waters and dropped it into a vat of other tangles like it. The murkiness dripped away like dross and the quicksilver re-liquefied.

chapter forty five

The Anannke greedily latched onto the attention of the now wild-eyed Thyaz, which blotted out his awareness of anything else. Every question Thyaz could think to ask was succinctly answered to the rat-a-tat of bare feet on the burnished metal that had replaced wood, stone and glass.

"Your true name was bastardized- Thyaz does not mean gifting, as you were told. You mocked the concept that in the eyes of those who raised you because… your penchant for thievery is tied to your stolen state of grace that- never mind- They knew what you were to be called… and chose the misnomer."

"Prior to descent ... Your true name was along the lines of

Theomachy- wars, heavenly, rebellion even, to those initiated- You were to be what might have been seen as a guerrilla warfare expert-" the Anannke prattled on, stroking his ego as if it were the feather crusted apron she'd adorned him with. The Anannke reproached Thyaz over her shoulder, as if hurt by his ignorance. "This dumbfounded, awestruck posturing is beneath you-I have always communicated with you-"

"It's the visual thing I guess-" Thyaz huffed awkwardly as he ran after the Anannke. "I never thought about what God looked like-" he said candidly. Fate and Thyaz turned a corner and stopped short. Fate's impassive mask shifted in shock at the sight of the one who'd lagged behind them crumpled on the floor in front of them, naked, trying to stand.

"What the fuck?" Thyaz grunted, bewildered by Artyo somehow being in front of them instead of right behind him.

Artyo bared her teeth at the Anannke. "What-where -?!" Artyo snarled. "WHAT IS this PLACE?" Her arm slashed angrily down the metallic hall, head cloudy, unable to make sense of the dark fog that seemed to press against her eyes from the inside out.

"Artyo! Are you-" Thyaz's words were blocked like lead blacks out the back of a mirror.

"Ascension sickness. It is to be expected," the Anannke tittered perfunctorily and continued down the hall. "One must Move through it."

"Where are we?" Artyo hissed again. Her wet eyes danced across the huge hexagon of fine mesh closest to her right as something behind it moved. Artyo's head continued to spin, only steadied by the shock that had flinched across the face of Fate upon them finding her.

Thyaz pulled her to him as if nothing had happened. "It's just ascension sickness," he parroted as he wiped spittle from her face. He felt her shake softly but didn't know what else to do but to follow Fate.

He pulled her forward in dazed pursuit of the Anannke. Worries about something having happened to Artyo when she was separated from him fought against the awareness that he hadn't even noticed her absence.

Be prepared to cut your losses echoed in his head but he waved it off, happy to at least have the pretense of Artyo's presence and laughed off the foreboding. They were in Heaven! And the Anannke really was The higher power he could now admit he'd missed all his life on Earth.

Artyo saw his heart in the flustered look in his eyes as he ambled after the Anannke like a love-struck puppy, desiring Fate itself more than he'd ever let himself long for her. He was never going to change, and to continue meant she'd always be this nakedly exhausted beside him. Even accessing some semblance of Heaven alongside her still hadn't been enough. The beauty of the last life and death had between them flooded out of her. She let the peace they'd passed through on the other side of hell on earth underscore what jostled roughly to the forefront of her heart.

Their story was done.

Til Death do ye part finally became real to her on a cellular level as soon as the last of her had been raised above the head of the Reaper cloaked being by the throat and flung to the ground. Everything after that moment in this place was a dark, sticky, nightmare-ish fog drowned in until the clarity of the twisted here and now.

It was the only loving thing to do. Give him over to the dicey fate he'd angrily longed to give a fuck for him his entire existence. Fate sprinted away again.

Artyo's hand slipped from his as Thyaz continued to run blindly after the Anannke. Artyo crashed to her knees again as they disappeared and the buzzing of the place suddenly overwhelmed her again.

The pitch went higher. She screamed out hoarsely and clawed at her ears until she could take no more. She bashed her head violently on the ground until everything went black.

chapter forty six

The smell of Kagome-Arachne's bloodletting bloomed in the dome. Crying that had gotten trapped in throats due to the interlopers' entry to her lair boomed, egged on by the squawking of giant, petulant black birds.

Kagome-Arachne effortlessly jumped over to the uppermost ledge of her zone to the huge nests the crows deposited surreptitiously carried, defiant souls into the Empyrean in that she'd stared into blankly for what felt like eons. The children looked up at the crazed spiderwoman warily, prepared to fight back.

"It's okay now. Don't worry. I remember you now. You're safe here. For the time being," Kagome-Arachne whispered. "I'll get you to where you desire to be, as promised. By Kagome-Arachne~" she purred with a flourish. Her spiritual blood gushed down her outstretched arms like crushed rubies and danced from her fingertips, splattering onto the foreheads of the bruised, crying children within the gigantic twists of branches.

It instantly soothed and sealed each face it spread over, cloaking whomever was under it. Calmed and relieved, the children smeared the ancient blood on the faces of all of the kids nearby and fell asleep for the first time after life.

chapter forty seven

Thyaz slammed his eyes shut to the white strands that whirled around him on his wild run after the gossamer wings of Fate. When he stopped running blind a wave of vertigo roughly sucker-punched the last bit of rarefied air out of him.

He was utterly lost.

He heaved, grasping backwards for a wall that wasn't there and swooned. He drunkenly flung himself face forward. Eyes flickered on the far side of the mesh as they watched him.

Clouds of incense rolled in, the resin scented smoke churning around him as he fell down in slow motion. He felt himself fighting for a consciousness that was wispier with each tendril of thought he struggled to hold onto. Silence settled in and unconsciousness prevailed.

 In a flash they scurried out, looking over their shoulders cravenly before they grabbed him and dragged him in.

chapter forty eight

Fate floated through the inner gardens of her complex inspecting the smallest new arrivals in utero. The bemused Anannke forgot about the presence of the interlopers as soon as the weight of their eyes on her vanished.

With the slightest nods to the stately Bodhis instructing the forcibly docile children, those that had obviously somehow arrived together were separated and scolded for any residual tears that flooded out like they had wet themselves during nap-time.

The removed fell in line behind the Anannke like abandoned chicks latching on to a new mother as she made her rounds. Some of them were re-delineated at the slightest wave of the Anannke's hand while others remained magnetized to her energetic wake.

They unconsciously began to levitate just like her as the last of what could only be called emotions drifted up and out of them through the pores of not yet scourged skin covering their Achilles heels. With each inhalation they lost more of themselves until even names could be re-assigned if needed, as was the norm upon following Fate.

"You become what Fate calls you~"

Eventually the remaining chickadee children were deposited in front of honeycombs of mesh deep within the complex.

They remained in place as silently instructed, stoic until the time arrived for them to be pulled over unspoken on thresholds for what could only be called sacrifice, although none within the Empyrean realm functioned with any understanding the word.

The Anannke did not look back at the offerings placed for what Fate could never admit was raised within the bowels of her purification complex to facilitate it.

The door closed behind her. Hallowed lights in the hall flickered as feeding time was announced by her exodus.

chapter forty nine

Thyaz came to in the center of a ring of stunningly beautiful Japanese women. They clapped like sweet little children when he finally stirred.

His face twisted up in confusion as each face clarified itself to him.

He did know them. All. Every single one of them.

He'd used them all. To varying degrees, royally slumming in both New York's and Tokyo's underground. But they didn't know each other. He'd always made sure of that. He always had just been that good.

The submissive women danced around the table together, each caressing him in her own special way that only the two of them would recognize. It was the slightest one who first noticed that his response to her touch was exactly the same as it had been to the two who had touched him before her.

"Liar! Cheat!" she screamed as she dug her nails into his thigh. "Uzostky! Byshunfu!"she thundered, "Lazy son of a-"

All the stroking screeched to a halt.

Thyaz sat up nervously as they looked at one another. The truth dawned on them all, all at once.

"No- I can explain- Ladies, I can- No! Please-please understand I-" he stammered.

His words got caught in his throat as the thunderer slammed her hand through his flesh. He screamed as she raised her bloody hand to her lips and licked it. He screeched in horror as the women swarmed him and tore him apart.

He passed out, only to wake back up within the ring of them swanning around him like numbers marching around a clock again and again, more cognizant of what the women he'd sucked the life out of were going to do to him each and every time. Payback literally was a ring of pissed off submissive bitches, just like he always used to say.

Fingers violently jabbed into his eye sockets to silence him and his bleating cries.

chapter fifty

The last bunch of kids left lining the synapse-like hallways in splendid outfits of red, blue and green trembled. Only children who could still rightly see knew what peered at them through the honeycombed mesh, waiting.

The teeth of the children began to chatter in unison, a twisted Morse code crying out for help they had never had on Earth. The scent of their adrenaline was a Pavlonian bell to the beasts behind the grids.

Suddenly all chattering stopped, throwing what waited across the thresholds for a loop long enough to pause them.

The little girl farthest down the line dropped to her knees in telepathic prayer. Heads whipped up back to the very first kid left behind by the Anannke as one after another they all silently followed suit, closing their eyes.

Tiny faces twisted up under pressure as they squeezed their souls for memories hidden deep within that they could use. The last little girl deposited reopened her eyes narrowly and balled up her fists.

Like a row of dominoes, all those chosen by Fate as food did the same.

Alarmed, the beasts on the other side of the mesh stepped back nervously as the children charged violently into their zones without one fear-soaked battle-cry uttered.

The hallowed light overhead flickered again as the atmosphere popped.

chapter fifty one

Thyaz flinched when he came to again, waving away rightfully vicious women that were no longer there.

His eyes steadied on a saturated stretch of sky that felt familiar to every cell in his body.

Tall grass waved into his line of sight as the black xylocopa mordax carpenter bees of his childhood lazily swam on the warm currents above him.

He was on his back in a field, one he'd once known to be bountiful via word of mouth as a child but had never seen in bloom due to the famine that had hit on the heels of his arrival.

Music danced above the crops and brought tears to his eyes.

Because he remembered.

Every single note of it. She'd played it the entire time they'd been carried and had it on as she went into labor.

Thyaz sat up sobbing in the tropical heat, bewildered by what kind of hellish heaven this place was.

He rose against his will, pulled by Tim Buckley's Song to the Siren blasting on repeat from the sprawling plantation house in the Dominican Republic that he was born in.

He heard his mother's screams of pain before he saw her through the window, saw her pushing with all of her might to get them through to no avail.

The two of them paced back and forth in the spirit beside the bed, holding hands, fighting to be there together.

Cherubim. Best friends forever, made of the same stars millions of years ago, finally able to be siblings. Twins. A one in a million shot.

He saw his fingers slip from hers as he slid through the veil, saw them screaming for each other, her promising to find him as the connection splintered and he screamed to life on earth.

He saw his waiting family crowd around his mother as the little girl who'd been all he'd had before here curled up in a ball in the corner and shook, screaming she'd find him until she disappeared.

He was the last of nine.

They were supposed to be ten. They'd buried his twin sister's body in that field and the field had turned fallow because she hadn't stayed there, had spirited away, in search of another road in.

Those dead fields were what had led to his father leaving his family behind in the Republic for New York City, had been why he'd married that horrible woman and had brought all nine of them up, one at a time into hell. Why he'd left their mother adrift all those years, having to trust that he could somehow morph back into the man she'd promised her life to after having given his life to someone else in search of a better life for them all.

It all came back in a flash and detonated in his chest. Watching the double life they'd all agreed to honor their father undertake as he'd lied to their stepmother every day. Taught him it was worth it, that a woman who loved him would put up with any desecration the world lobbed at her due to things he did, and there would never be any comeuppance to his bad behavior. It was just what men did.

Thyaz ran across his father's dead fields crying.

He'd forgotten.

Her.

He saw everything he'd put her through even after she'd kept her word and found him.

Saw that she'd found a way in and had hunted him down and he'd made her life a living hell every chance he had gotten. Because she could not behave like the woman she hadn't been able to even be born through.

The truth stabbed at what was left of him.

His legs gave out at the shore.

She'd always loved him.

Always. Before space. Beyond time.

And he'd forgotten.

Had lived life lashing out at it, had justified every fucked up thing he'd chosen to do to life as payback for never finding any actual love in it. Retaliation.

Most of which had landed on Artyo.

Unable to bear it, Thyaz walked into the ocean and drowned himself.

chapter fifty two

The stone-faced ANCs waited to be announced. The austerity of the Anannke's inner chamber read as an altar to their still-scaled eyes. The slubbed fabric encasing their legs matched the penance-scarred flesh of their bare backs. Their spindly fingers wrapped around the ankles of a blacked out Artyo suspended between the two of them as they waited for instructions.

To them Artyo was no more than that moment's sacrifice.

The Anannke sat with her back to them in the lotus pool, thoughts absently fixed on the outer reaches of her territory visible through the ripped out sections of granite that made up the farthest wall of her quarters. Waiting. For him to finally catch up. Across times, trials and purifying tribulations.

Specks of moisture pulsated across her chest as her mind processed the reality of what was in this particular now. The old lore dervished behind eyes the sentinels could not see.

The Anannke gingerly pressed her fingers along the strand of her long, white lock that was and would always be him and attempted to untangle it from the gnarled mess that was Artyo's without losing composure, well aware that Artyo was strung up like a pig behind her wet back.

The Anannke called on Sector. The download of all relevant information flooded into her, the feed flipping back and forth between Sector and the Anannke as if one was pressing oneself for answers.

"What shall they do with his One?" Sector asked aloud in the space for the benefit of the ANCs. The false filial piety of the ANCs had driven itself so deep into their cells that it rotted against the membranes of their scaled eyes in hollow shows of reverence and loyalty.

The Anannke looked absently over her shoulder at the neutered giants that held the ashen, naked and catatonic Artyo between them, showing surprisingly no interest in inspecting their prize.

The mark of the beast glowed on Artyo's shell, one that had been flagrantly left out in the open to be discovered. Daring Fate itself. Deep within its own zone. A declaration of War and she knew it. The Anannke remained silent, insulted by the audacious territorial foul and moved to something akin to fear. "Store her where it is obvious that neither of them belong to ensure he finds her."

The reverent ANCs nodded and exited the Anannke's quarters.

"Do you really feel that persuaded by the power inherent in the purified unity of these crumbs to stop what is coming? Even though this pocket we are now faced with squashing... out of... Necessity… obviously rose up in the wake of their disconnect?" Sector asked the Anannke plainly as he materialized in the shadows, his back to her.

"That there was even space for anything that could be read as "early" in all of this underscores the... Necessity... of tossing all cards to reveal the truth in the fire of fires. Here ...ahead of all prophesies and timetables is still somehow… Here." the Anannke murmured as her eyes adjusted to the spread of the shoulders of Sector in her personal space, a gift rarely granted.

Sector looked back at her and silently raised a mercurial brow at the Necessity of all things being forced to be ready to burn all cards.

"Spec to my logos. All directions. Now." the Anannke growled with a clip of superiority to her voice and looked through Sector out across the dominion ascribed to Fate.

Sector smirked softly, nodded in acceptance of the directive and eased out of her ocular purview, evaporating into the mists surrounding her.

The Anannke looked away and picked through the download alone.

chapter fifty three

Thyaz regained consciousness to the sound of churning water. Heat rose up from grates in the floor beside him, the first thing to register to his filmy eyes. He inched his body towards the sound of the water, cheek close to the floor like a drunk keeping his face cool against the porcelain of a toilet.

Upon contact he blindly dipped his cracked palms into the oscillating water then dragged them across his face. As his hands made their way back to the water for the second time, a breeze blew over him.

Thyaz pulled his head up in slow motion to find the Anannke seated in the pool of water full of lotus blooms, staring at him. A sigh of relief escaped him. Just as quickly the atmosphere thickened in his head as Artyo rose back up in his mind.

Horror plastered across his face as it registered that he had lost her and so quickly forgotten her in the light of the Anannke. "Oh my god-WHERE IS SHE-?!" he choked.

"Your impassioned realization of her absence does not conceal your abandonment of her to any involved parties." The Anannke spat venomously.

Dumbfounded, Thyaz felt the brush of Sector's sensory fibers across his flesh. He stumbled for words as he felt strategies being outlined against them. Every horrific end played itself out against the insides of his eyes accusingly, as if each and every one was Artyo's fate simultaneously, immobilizing any fight left in Thyaz. "Please-just tell me where she is-?" he barked softly, overwhelmed.

"The repentance is rather exemplary-" the Anannke muttered, "although over the top for my taste-and too late to be of any import."

Her tonality cut Thyaz to the quick. "Don't even -" he whispered dully, debilitated by the horror shows Sector mercilessly pummeled his mainframe with.

The Anannke tried to ignore a twist of what could only be called jealousy due to his concern for the woman he'd barreled into the afterlife to be with, but the antagonism was fully in her voice. Thyaz closed his eyes at the sound of Fate as it boomed.

"I am not in a place to tell you where your 'beloved' has washed up. I am also unable to stop your sure to be fruitless search for her. It seems you are integral to what brought her here in the first place. In ways beyond my interference."

The Anannke shifted in her bathing water as if the existence of Thyaz had suddenly erased itself from her radar. The gnosis he had chased after to the detriment of the one who had opened the door in the first place had left him without either. When he opened his eyes, there was nowhere to go but up.

"I'll find her myself-" he snarled softly and pulled himself up off the floor as the Anannke continued bathing. Thyaz made his way out of the quarters he had been dragged into eons earlier.

chapter fifty four

The lore sung out at the Anannke from the consciously destroyed walls within her chamber as she went into state. Her hair unfurled like wings and flooded out of the space into the vista beyond her quarters.

"Lost light-bringers return, impossible offspring in tow, rapture, councils, destroyed, too much curiosity festering in the Emp- interlopers, presence- Denizens is not helping matters. vanquished children, more rebellion with each passing day-"

"Entities-questioning faculties... Lowest primal expectations... goats must be provided… Debuted... presented to the Citizens and Denizens of the Empyrean -esteemed guest... or the root of all suddenly wrong within this fiery abode and eradicated-"

"And as for whom she-" the Anannke paused in her rant, "that will be the definer of all- but the hive must stop instruction... Eject all who are in process into the field."

"But they aren't ready." fate whispered to herself . "Apparently they are or this would not be in play-Do what is necessary..."

" Prepare for purification to spec."

chapter fifty five

Thyaz searched for Artyo, completely overcome with guilt. His body suddenly began to lurch forward, as if the synapses that had recorded him ingesting the drugs that took him out had been grazed. Thyaz played with believing this was all some sick insanity brought on by the Molotov cocktail of pharmaceuticals he had ingested set to Death Valley but knew better.

"Knowing her, she was as consciously clean as I was dirty when I bounced." he mumbled and looked around.

"Fuck it- she found me in New York City and Tokyo and I was able to find her in the guts of whatever the hell this fucking place actually is… and by my damned self, too... so I'll be able to find her now-" Thyaz muttered angrily to himself.

His heartbeat echoed in his ears as he searched through terraces full of graveyards choked with tipped over headstones, terrified he'd find her under one gasping for the life that couldn't be lost all the way up here so close to the fire.

He wheezed against the thick sweetness of the air as he ducked back indoors and made his way down yet another series of bizarre hallways he'd been too enraptured by Fate to have fully taken notice of before.

Images flickered in his peripheral vision and faded whenever he turned to focus on them. He walked on, his exhaustion and self-loathing spinning the more opulent the empty spaces alongside him became.

Rough, ore-scarred expanses of polished rock gave way to gold and silver plated rooms whose far walls had been ripped out to expose horizon lines full of chaotic landscapes he could not have comprehended if he had paused to take them in anyway.

Solitary chambers flitted past with Bodhis he couldn't see at altars to things they planned to worship if they ever got out, drunk off of what they imagined the lives they wanted their chance at would feel like.

Over-perfected entities hovered above pillows on their knees, faiths quickened by the passing scent of one who had been born where their every breath in the afterlife had them desiring to be.

The hot metal under his bare feet began to fade into cool copper veined marble as the narrow hallway he turned down doubled both in width and height every few steps into the dark space he suddenly found himself in.

He pushed past the fragile blockades that dissolved in utter shock at his insubordination and walked down an incline that felt familiar in the dark, which freaked him out more than anything else he'd experienced since arriving in this place. A sound echoed in the distance.

He picked his way forward in the dark. His fingers jammed into a carved marble box that suddenly made Thyaz think of ancient coffins museums in New York had before such places became off-limits to his kind.

A new feeling of dread coated him as he backed away and slammed into the sharp corner of another huge cold box behind him. He sprinted to the right and stumbled into coffin after coffin in a panic until the sound of scratching made him stop in his tracks.

Thyaz was so scared that his knuckles began to glow in the dark as he reached out and ran his fingers across the carved top of the stone box the scratching sound had to have come from. He found a groove about four inches below the rim. He began to push with all his might against the heavy slab until it moved about an inch. Thyaz inhaled harshly and collapsed against it. He leaned the side of his hot face against the cool stone and heard the sound of rushing water inside the box. He pushed until a slash of light erupted that momentarily hypnotized him with its clarity.

The scratching grew louder and snapped him out of his daze. The veins along his temples throbbed as he forced himself against the slab ferociously. More light shot up into the hangar. With one final shove, the cover was pushed a quarter of the way off of the stone sarcophagus. The sound of water boomed as he looked up at the ceiling and saw the white wispy hairs of the Anannke plastered to it. He looked down. The crest of a tiny wave of water broke against his foot. He pulled himself up onto the marble crate. Granite gargoyles suspended from buttresses along a stepped membrane glared down at the half-lit stretch of deepening metallic water that seemed to go on forever.

Bewildered, he swung his feet over into the brightness, looked around one last time, closed his eyes and ducked his face into the light. Air bubbles burst next to his ears full of Artyo's screams underwater.

In horror, Thyaz yanked his head up out of the blue light just as something came up behind him, rammed him back in and slammed the cover back into place over both of their screams.

chapter fifty six

The quicksilver waters rose around the marble faced wooden coffins.

They floated lazily upon its surface, gently careening into the other coffins as they bobbed towards the gigantic drop crater at the edge of the purification complex and plummeted down into the Empyrean, smashing from one atmosphere into the next.

Thrown by the sudden momentum of their fall, Thyaz lunged at Artyo and kissed her on the mouth underwater as they slammed arms around each other and locked eyes, prepared to be the last thing either would ever see, finally.

The boxes exploded on impact around the seven sacred Empyrean pools where baptisms into the realm were held once the purification process was over. Wherever the corpses landed across the zone delineated the levels of untouchable bliss allotted post-puryf, upon being allowed to move freely within the realm.

The corpses of Artyo and Thyaz officially arrived in the Empyrean cleaved to one another when their broken bodies floated up to the surface of the first of the sacred pools of bloodied water, dead flesh bruised by the shrapnel of marble and wood.

chapter fifty seven

Re-calibration diagnostics began with a flash of ultraviolet light.

Attendants came at broken bodies from all directions, whispering softly as hands tried to pry the two of them apart.

Artyo began screaming. A voice warned Thyaz that they would not be separated unless she couldn't calm down, only re-calibrated for ease of entry into the Empyrean realm.

Thyaz grabbed Artyo and groggily begged her to calm down between cold kisses intended to comfort her as she dug her nails into his neck. Voices kept telling them that neither of them would be hurt, to not be afraid. The physical trauma of descension cleaved them tightly together. Physical infinity grated against the moralities of offended attendants who helmed the diagnostics, Purificationists who had long since burnt such human necessities out of their systems.

Their bodies were forcibly pulled apart in disgust. They both kicked and screamed, unable to see anything except being yanked out of each other's reach. Thyaz went hoarse screaming for Artyo as they were strapped onto glass tables full of tiny holes angled at thirty three degrees. Their vision began to re-set after they were partially sedated.

They watched each other like hawks. Lulled by the voices moving around him, Thyaz suddenly was overwhelmed by exhaustion. Artyo watched him fall asleep warily, knowing it'd be impossible for any of the hustler in him to do so if they were not safe. Artyo's thoughts froze as the voices that had been blocked out by her screams kneaded her brain. She fought grogginess, lids heavy, refusing to fully close her eyes for fear of them taking Thyaz away from her.

Bark, charcoal and ash were rubbed across them to ensure the potent drugs applied afterwards would easily be absorbed. Attendants scrubbed them with salts and oils until they gleamed and then filed out of the space. The ceiling opened and red light flooded the re-calibration room. The top layer of flesh was burnt off by the atmosphere of the realm itself, devouring years off the interlopers.

Hair was washed in copper basins after the ceiling closed, then oiled, painted with protective silk fibers and sheathed. Torrential downpours of honeyed water healed infrared burns across their skins. A trickle of liquid mercury dripped down onto each forehead. It slowly coated them to the tips of their toes before it seeped in, leaving behind a quicksilver web that mirrored nerves beneath their flesh, amplifying the perfected gloss they already were burnished to. The tables were pushed together again. To the shocked chagrin of the attendants they still absently reached for each other. They curled around one another in the fetal position as they slept. Hair blended together and made a halo around them as tiny beads of moisture on the silk filaments caught the light.

The tables were lowered to 180 degrees then submerged in paraffin wax before being returned to their original angles. The excess wax drained through the holes and hardened around them, then was peeled off.

She shoved him softly to wake him up. He shoved her back to let her know he hadn't been sleeping. If they hadn't become so good at ignoring everything outside of them they'd have seen their eyes had completely adjusted to the vibration of the realm, the beings milling around them and the trails of residual light left when they moved. She'd have felt the menacing press of the eyes of First and Second Head piercing through her and an unmistakable alarm would have sounded.

"Just Protocol," Attendants whispered, explaining the details of the next step in the process to them in hushed tones.

"You are to go under separately, but in lotus pools facing one another."

Naked except for white loincloths, they were oblivious to the crowd that had gathered to witness the first double diagnostic ever performed in the realm.

Artyo and Thyaz were led down a hall of chinowa rings of lashed together reeds to the baptismal pools and stood face to face, steadied by the sight of one another.

"You're ready?" Thyaz smirked.

"No," Artyo murmured, "You?"

"Course not...but what else is there to do? I mean, I'm good, long as I keep getting to jump with you-" Thyaz whispered.

The Attendants closest to them cleared their throats.

They separated them, then stood them facing one another with the distance of two pools between them. They looked down at water the color and consistency of India ink. As their bodies were eased down the water began to spin. Artyo's mouth dropped open in surprise and she tried with all her might to keep her eyes locked on Thyaz as the water whirled clockwise for her. Her mind's eye calmed when it focused on the fact that he found her at the last moment in the Per-A complex.

The warm, black water rising spun counter-clockwise for Thyaz but he refused to look down. They were steered into the center of their respective pools in silence, closer together. Eyes locked on each other, they were dunked beneath the churning surface.

chapter fifty eight

Gavels dropped in distant corridors echoed throughout the sound-systems of the Empyrean realm. The fate of the two interlopers was decided by official re-routing votes upon immersion.

The hummingbirds and dragon-flies that had danced above the surface of the water, the only unspeakable delight given to those who sat in silence through the re-calibration alongside the submerged two dispersed at the sound of the echoing judgment.

Confused quasi-heretics silently rooting for them and unable to believe what had just been pirate broadcast watched the scene aghast.

Denizens who'd revealed unclean hearts by their presence alone turned away from the impossible thoughts trying to gain footholds in their minds regarding the retribution that awaited them within their cells for hoping against hope.

Confused , the Denizens and Borderlines that had quietly lined the edges of the pools threw in handfuls of brightly colored flowers and woodenly left offerings of beautiful fruit they had lost desire to eat upon arrival in the Empyrean as they solemnly filed away. Wild grasses with scents that meant nothing there that had been tied into rings of hope were also left behind along with bolts of luxurious fabrics that felt like sandpaper to numbed out Denizen fingers.

The last heretics dejectedly rose up from their lotus poses and walked away, destroyed and unable to let it show.

chapter fifty nine

Artyo came to floating under the surface of murky water, her body bobbing in the direction it spun. She went to raise her head and felt it get sternly pushed back down into the water.

Something deep inside her made her push up against the arms she could now see were holding her down. She lashed at them the best that she could underwater, kicking and screaming, fighting. The struggle just made more water flood into her lungs all the faster. They held her thrashing body underwater until she drowned.

The bruised Baptizers of Artyo silently trudged out of the lotus pool and flicked the water off of their hands dispassionately as the marched single file beside the chinowa rings back into the complex.

Her body was left floating in the waters the last of life had been squeezed out of her in for what would have been thirty-nine days in a realm were there was a night and day.

On the fortieth day, perfected women marched in with a giant Chinese chicken coop basket carried between the six of them. They solemnly eased themselves into the water, slid the basket under Artyo, sunk under the surface of the lotus pool and lifted the basket they'd carried on their hips together onto their shoulders. Their feet re-connnected with the polished stairs of the pool and they carried a waterlogged Artyo out of it up towards the place she belonged, an overflow of blackwater trailing behind them due to the open weave of the basket she'd been retrieved in.

chapter sixty

Off in distant places in his mind, Thyaz heard the faint wailing of someone he knew to be utterly afraid of water, yet couldn't place a name to the face being slowly yet fully erased from his head. He fell asleep, oblivious to the fact that he was being held underwater until the last life was drowned out of him.

What once would have been forty days passed.

Thyaz beatifically opened his eyes floating in the glistening, black water to find a red sky overhead.

The Retrievers slid into the lotus pool and he was raised overhead from the depths without being touched, utterly reborn.

He walked on water towards the lip of the lotus pools, away from anchoring energies that had once been and was led down glowing corridors in silent revelry as the sounds of the Empyrean crested on sweet winds around his numb and naked frame, totally washed of all memories.

chapter sixty one

The kid sat still as possible, unnoticed in the meat grinder of energy crushing everything around her it could get its teeth into.

She pulled the thrifted gray beanie she'd doused for 25 cents in the summer that had turned out to be cashmere further down on her forehead, still amazed that it worked just like the New Caledonian crone had said.

The nimbus of protective energy around her shook as the spirit of a nearby adult crashed to the ground less than three feet away, pounced on by what had hounded her from the time her feet had hit the floor.

The woman stood there listlessly watching the demons she thought only she could see claw at the best she thought she had to give in broad daylight, unaware of the capped little kid peering through a tangle of hair behind her. She'd witnessed every different part of herself dying for so long that it almost didn't matter. Every new attack was a surprise, a speck of sanity she didn't realize she'd still had until watching it die. Suddenly her cold clammy skin began to crawl like she was being watched.

"Steady," the little kid muttered.

She narrowed her eyes in alarm as one of the lady's demons whipped one of its heads up from its feast and sniffed the air ravenously. The girl hunched down deeper between her shoulders and prayed for strange breezes and bells that always showed up just in time.

The broken woman retched as the hungry ghost stepped into her. She snarled with a hatchet face sixty years older than she actually was.

The kid sucked air through her teeth and prayed for rain as she watched the remnant of the woman's soul fight for panicked dominion over her body right before her eyes.

Out of nowhere the wind kicked up. The kid hunkered down as the wind went so wild that it set off car alarms nearby, startling both the beasts and the woman out of the spiritual fight just enough for her to gain the upper hand. The wind rushed around the haggard lady and beat back the spiritual beasts that had been upon her.

The still standing woman dropped to her knees crying over the bruised and broken splinter of herself in the street as she scooped her up, apologizing for forgetting about the aspect as she hugged her back into herself.

The winds stopped. She looked up, saw the kid staring gape-mouthed at her, no clue to the angelic beings evaporating one by one around her that had arrived like a torrent and beat back her demons.

All she saw was a dirty kid in a wool hat in the summer, watching her almost breakdown as she waited for the bus.

The kid looked away as the woman wiped at her tears with the back of her hand and awkwardly turned to go.

The bus came.
The kid got on and then off, spooked.
She'd never seen them before, had only felt them. The Angels. Now she knew they were as real as the demons she'd seen since birth.

She absently pulled the mail out of the rusty mailbox she'd nervously checked every day to no avail.

It was there.

Her hands shook as she held it up to her big brother, their mother nowhere to be found as usual.

He understood. He was already there. For years now.
She followed him into the kitchen.

"It's thin-" he muttered, holding it up to the light as the teapot screamed. "Can't remember if that's good or bad-"

He ran the envelope back and forth in the steam escaping the spout and gingerly pried the envelope open as the little kid gripped the table with bony, little calloused fingers.

He extracted the letter and grunted as he read each sentence to himself. She felt struck by each noise he made, too on the edge of death to scream at him for drawing it out.

He looked down at his cagey, combative little beast of a sister who was too terrified to be triggered into smacking him like she'd been taught to by him for messing with her and decided to stop the torment.

He sighed with disgust.

"I guess you're riding the bus with me next week because Arts finally let you -"

She burst into tears and bear-hugged her big brother for the first time in years, smearing happy snot all over his t-shirt.

"IN-ugh man! Dang!" he laughed, trying not to cry too.

She was the only one of the kids in the house who'd actually had talent, and the last of them to get into Arts after trying for eons in the major she'd wanted instead of all the other departments that had continually accepted her in lieu of it.

He hugged her back until she calmed down.
"You good?" he mumbled. She nodded. He playfully shoved her off of him. She burst out laughing.

"Gone- go tell everybody-" he laughed.

The kid ran out onto the porch, jumped up on the banister and roared at the top of her melodic little lungs to her neighborhood like the town crier she was.

"I GOT INTO ARTS! I GOT INTO ARTS!!!" she yelled.

Howls, screams, cheers and laughter erupted in their weird little pocket of peace holding its own in Hell on Earth.

"Congratulations, baby!" her tiny, ancient neighbors sung back to her as she jumped up and down before happily running back into the house.

The End.

ABOUT THE AUTHOR

Author and multimedia artist Angel Brynner has marched to the beat of her
own drum across the arts for over two decades. After formal training with
the vanguard of the menswear industry she helmed her own line of men's
clothing and produced events for the collection in the club scenes of
New York and Tokyo.

She became quietly known for the futuristic cautionary tales back-dropping
her collections, taking over clubs and the guerilla-marketing style she used
to slam her vision into the hearts of her fans. While being sponsored by
Multinational companies desiring audience with her underground tribe, she
returned from Japan to her hometown to press charges against a pedophile
before the statute of limitations ran out.

Cast as a vigilante by a corrupt sex crimes unit for trying to protect another
child from the same attacker, during the media onslaught against
the first brave adults to come forward and press charges against
the Catholic priests that had abused them as children she was hit with a
vision of all those already lost in a sick war on kids no one talked about.
She committed herself & her art to doing something about it.
The grievechronic universe was forged in the fires of imagining the
Armageddon that would erupt through a generation of kids who
had finally had enough abuse at the hands of adults and
banded together under their grievances.
The epic spiritual, metaphysical, and historical implications
of such an event played out on every level- from the hellish norms
that caused it to what would be called heaven by such a broken world-
made her head spin..
Alongside AOLAB[the active-art series featuring the multimedia work
that fed Eutaxis, Ecclesia, Exodus, Erebus, Exist and the kinetic collection
of novels that follow them], Angel Brynner's books are the culmination of
an artistic journey many years in the making,
all leading to a mysterious future project entitled Transcendence.

Eutaxis
/grievechronic\
Angel Brynner
Ecclesia
/grievechronic\
Angel Brynner
Exodus
/grievechronic\
Angel Brynner

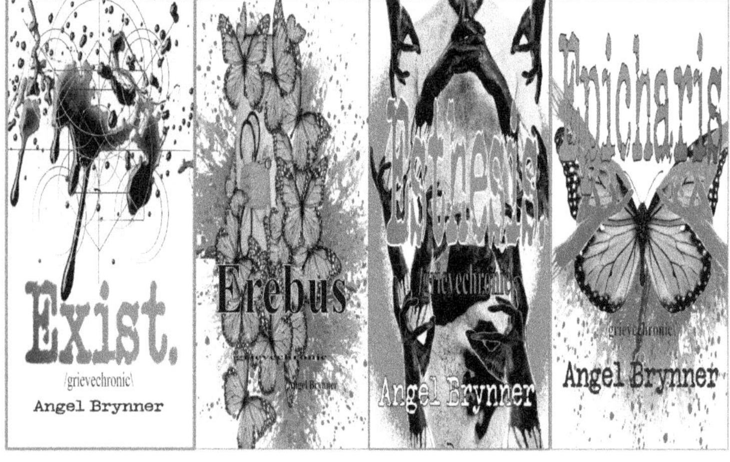

Exist.
/grievechronic\
Angel Brynner
Erebus
/grievechronic\
Angel Brynner
/grievechronic\
Angel Brynner
Epicharis
/grievechronic\
Angel Brynner

...Want more?

Email info@kokopellimapress.com
For access to exclusive, free and
special edition goods tied to all things
Angel Brynner / AOLAB \ Globalboho.
...and check out www.grievechronic.com

www.ingramcontent.com/pod-product-compliance
Lightning Source LLC
Chambersburg PA
CBHW061308210726
48293CB00003B/1163